# HIGHLAND

# FOLK
# TALES

# HIGHLAND
# FOLK
# TALES

BOB PEGG

The History Press

First published 2012

The History Press
The Mill, Brimscombe Port
Stroud, Gloucestershire, GL5 2QG
www.thehistorypress.co.uk

Reprinted 2012

© Bob Pegg, 2012

British Library Cataloguing in Publication Data.
A catalogue record for this book is available from the British Library.

ISBN 978 0 7524 6090 1

Typesetting and origination by The History Press
Printed in Great Britain by TJ Books Limited, Padstow, Cornwall

# CONTENTS

# Acknowledgements

My old friend and long-time collaborator John Hodkinson has, as ever, surpassed expectation with his bold illustrations.

Alec Williamson and Essie Stewart are great sources of inspiration. Both have generously given permission for their stories to be used here, and their contributions are credited where they occur throughout the book.

Thanks to Dolly MacDonald for her Seaboard memories.

Jenny Neesham first acquainted me with the story of The Flying Princess in 1981, and later gave me a copy of David Thomson's *The People of the Sea*, which I had very much in mind when working on this book.

The late Hugh MacNally's telling of Angie and the Calf and Angus Grant's recollections of Jimmy the Dolphin originally appeared on the recording 'From Sea to Sea', released by The Highland Council in 2001.

The Boy and the Blacksmith is © of The Estate of Duncan Williamson, and is used by kind permission of Linda Williamson.

Isabella Ross kindly gave permission to use the family story of The Bodach Stabhais.

Flora Fullarton Pegg reminded me of The Story of Fergus Smith, which I once told, but had entirely forgotten.

Martin and Frieda Gostwick gave invaluable help with the chapter Miller's World of Wonders and put me right on the fine details of Hugh Miller's life.

I'm grateful to Isabel Henderson for first making me aware of the story of The Desert Fathers, and inviting me to tell it in Nigg Church, where images from the story are carved into a Pictish cross-slab.

George Adams of Helmsdale passed on information about fishermen's superstitions.

The photograph on the back of the cover is by Fergus Fullarton Pegg.

The receipt of a Creative Scotland storytelling bursary in 2010, for the project Walking the Stories, helped enormously in my exploration of the links between story and landscape in the Highlands.

Finally, my thanks to Mairi MacArthur, not only for her help with Gaelic spelling and pronunciation, but for her unstinting support throughout the writing of *Highland Folk Tales*.

# Introduction

In 1989 I moved from North Yorkshire to the Scottish Highlands. I came to live in Hilton, one of the Seaboard villages on the Nigg peninsula in Easter Ross. The three communities that make up the villages – Shandwick, Balintore and Hilton itself – thread round a bay in an unbroken string of white dwellings. They are old settlements. Their names, present and past, derive both from Gaelic and from Old Norse. In Gaelic, Balintore is Baile an Todhair, the bleaching town. For the Vikings, Shandwick was a sandy bay, and Cadboll, in the region of Hilton, was the farm of the cats. Out in the bay south of Shandwick is a rock shelf known as the King's Sons, where local tradition holds that three Viking princes drowned when they came seeking revenge against the Earl of Ross for his cruel treatment of their sister.

The Nigg peninsula is known particularly for the three great sculpted slabs that once stood in Hilton, Shandwick and Nigg (the Hilton stone is now in the National Museum of Scotland in Edinburgh, and was replaced by a replica, carved by Barry Grove, in 2000). At one time people believed that the stones had been erected to commemorate the three Viking princes who perished out in the bay. We now know that they were carved by the Picts, some time around the ninth century. They show hunting scenes, bestiaries, trumpeters, a harp, a woman apparently riding side-saddle, together with elaborately ornamented crosses and an array of symbols whose meanings have never been convincingly interpreted. In 1996 the discovery of the site of a Pictish monastery at Portmahomack, at the north-east tip of the peninsula, made it plain why such impressive Christian cross-slabs would be found close by.

One evening early in my first January in Hilton I saw fire, miles away on the far side of the Moray Firth. It was years later that I realised I must have glimpsed the Burghead Clavie, a rare survivor of what, not so long ago, were widespread midwinter fire parades. In Burghead, a blazing tar barrel is carried around the village – the site of a Pictish fort – on the shoulders of local men. Some believe that the Clavie is a survival from pagan times, a vital ceremony designed to ensure the return of light in the middle of winter darkness; it's a fitting, if romantic, belief, in a place whose latitude is further north than that of Moscow, and whose winters can be long and hard.

The Seaboard villages can seem more isolated than the apparently more remote communities of the West Highlands, even though they are only a few miles off the A9, the main road to the north. Twenty years ago, the majority of the inhabitants were people whose families had lived there at least since the nineteenth century, the times of the Highland Clearances, when they had been evicted from their crofts in Sutherland, and Gaelic was still the first language of a handful of the older folk. They were the last generation of native speakers in the East Highlands, apart from some members of the Traveller community who still speak it today; though even among the Travellers it has almost died out.

One of the native Gaelic speakers in the village when I first arrived was Cathy Ross (there were many Rosses in the Seaboard). She was a tiny little lady who had never married, and who lived in a small, immaculately kept cottage just along Shore Street. Every day she would pass by my front door, taking a walk round the block for exercise, and would always stop to chat. The older inhabitants of Hilton knew her as 'Toy'.

Dolly MacDonald, another Hilton dweller, was of a generation younger than Toy. I would often see her walking Mac, her West Highland Terrier, along the path between my garden and the beach. One morning I was sitting out in the sun playing the melodeon – an old-fashioned squeeze box. Dolly came towards me along the path, with Mac trotting beside her. She stopped by the gate and danced a little jig to the music. 'My mother used to have one of those,' she said, meaning the melodeon. 'There was a lot of music around when we were bairns.' She began to talk about the old times, and told me the story of a young man who lived in Balintore. 'Did you hear of him?' she said.

This is how I remember Dolly's story. The young man was walking along Shandwick beach one day when he saw in the distance a merrymaid – that was Dolly's name for a mermaid – sitting on a rock. She was very beautiful and he thought she looked as if she'd make a good wife, but he wondered how he could stop her going back to the sea. He remembered something he'd heard – that if you find a merrymaid sitting on a rock and you walk around the rock three times widdershins, her tail will fall away. He thought he'd give it a try. He walked round the rock three times, and indeed her tail did drop off, and she had a good pair of legs underneath it.

The young man grabbed the tail and ran back to his cottage. He went to the shed at the bottom of the garden, folded the tail up and hid it behind the plant pots. Then he went into the kitchen and waited. Well, eventually he saw the merrymaid coming up the road, getting used to her land legs. She knocked at his door. When he answered it she asked for her tail back. He wouldn't give it to her, but he did invite her in. They shared a pot of tea and got on quite well together and soon they were married, and in time they had three children.

She was a good mother but she missed her life in the sea. One day the man woke up and there was no sign of the merrymaid. He went down the garden to the shed and looked behind the plant pots, and the tail had gone. Of course she must have found it and slipped it back on and returned to the sea. That was the last the man and the three children ever saw of her.

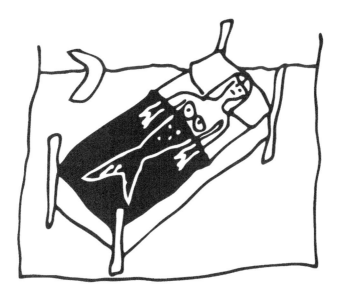

That was Dolly's story. I had heard something like it before, told not about a mermaid but a selkie girl. The selkies, whom we'll meet again later, are shape-changers. They are seals who can become human on land by taking off their skins. The story was about a young man who stole a selkie's skin, so that she was forced to marry him; it became so popular in the late twentieth century that it was made into a children's picture book, and became a feminist parable, in which a woman has to choose between her family and her true nature. But tellings of it were always set in a misty Celtic past. Dolly's story took place just down the road in Balintore, some time within the past few years. The young man himself might still be living, perhaps remarried to a Seaboard girl.

The Highlands are no Arcadia. They famously have a turbulent, often cruel past, and are beset today by the same kinds of social problems and personal fears that afflict other parts of Britain. But hearing Dolly MacDonald tell the story of the merrymaid so casually that summer morning made me realise that I had come to live in a place where old folk tales were still living and breathing, and were part of the landscape and the life of communities.

On one occasion, I had an experience so strange that it felt as if I was actually in one of these stories. Among the many snippets of local lore that Dolly passed on was that there was a family in the Seaboard who were 'off the seals', meaning that, like the renowned MacCodrums of South Uist, their lineage had been enriched by a liaison between humans and the people of the sea.

November 5th was a big date in the Seaboard calendar. Small fires were lit in gardens and in streets throughout the villages, but there were two big bonfires, one in Balintore, the other in Hilton, and there was great rivalry between the supporters of each. The house of one of my close neighbours, a retired naval man, overlooked the field where the Hilton bonfire was stacked high, and he had taken it upon himself to keep watch, to make sure the Balintore boys didn't sneak in and set it alight before the allotted time. When the evening of the 5th arrived, the Hilton field reeled in a bacchanal of explosions and merriment, with schoolchildren, matrons, respectable village tradespeople and shrieking teenage girls weaving round each other, and men brandishing half bottles staggering through the smoke. My neighbour was also the official lighter of fireworks. When the last Roman Candle had expired, and the bonfire was down to glowing ash, he beckoned me into his back garden. The old seadog had managed to procure a bottle of Pusser's rum, which he had hidden in the garden – but had apparently hidden so well that we couldn't find it at all (later we discovered that his wife had been there before us, had found the bottle and confiscated it).

'Never mind,' he said, 'I know where there'll be a drink.' I followed him back into the field, over stone walls and down little paths for what seemed like miles, until we climbed over a fence into someone's back garden. Without knocking, the sober sailor entered, with me close behind. In the kitchen, round a big wooden table, sat a group of people who all had round, pale faces and big brown eyes. I felt as if I was the seal killer entering the kingdom of the selkie folk – his story is told later. Surely these were the people Dolly had spoken of. Whether or not they were off the seals, we were shown great hospitality and they were warm company, though I never did meet any of them again.

Seven years after I came to the Highlands, early in the summer of 1996, Mairi MacArthur and I were in Thin's bookshop in Inverness, for the launch of Timothy Neat's book *The Summer Walkers*. The book gathers together the spoken autobiographies of some of the Scottish Travelling people, together with wonderful photographs of the Travellers and their campsites. Two of the book's subjects were at the launch: Alec Williamson, who had settled in Edderton, where his family used to winter when they were still on the road; and Essie Stewart who, at that time, was living in Inverness, but in earlier days had travelled Sutherland and Caithness with her adoptive mother Mary, and her grandfather, the renowned Gaelic storyteller Ailidh Dall, Blind Sandy Stewart. Tim talked about the book, and then Alec was invited to sing a song in Gaelic. The big voice, from the big man, filled Thin's, and the ghosts of campfires began to glow among the well-ordered shelves.

You will meet Alec and Essie again, and find out more about their remarkable lives and the tales they heard when they were young. Both of them are still telling those stories, in the festivals and community events which have sprung from a recent international revival of interest in storytelling. In this collection, I have tried to reflect the spirit of that revival. I have heard, or have told, all the stories here. Most are given in my own words, but if readers would like to explore other versions – and there are many – some references are given in the Afterword.

Many of the stories are very old, and have travelled widely, taking root in different cultures and adjusting to the languages of those cultures with ease. This adaptability has led to their settling down comfortably in particular places, often embracing topographical features and their names, and sometimes incorporating the names of families and individuals from these places. I've reflected this attachment to location by arranging most of the stories along the routes of journeys, which can either be taken in the imagination, or through the physical landscape of the Highlands.

The stories are at their best told out loud. This is an invitation to take your favourites, to make them yours and pass them on in your own words, just as storytellers have done for thousands of years.

*Bob Pegg, 2012*

# WOOD AND WATER

The Drumochter Pass, which rises a little over 1,500ft above sea level, is officially where the Highlands begin. In the middle of winter it's more barrier than gateway. The worst of the snows will close the pass, forcing drivers heading north up the A9 to make a massive detour round the east coast, by Dundee and Aberdeen. Even on the finest summer day there is a sense of leaving the modern world behind – the galleries and theatres of Edinburgh, the cosmopolitan eating places of Glasgow – and entering another country, where human affairs are dwarfed by the capaciousness of the landscape, and giants would be the most appropriate inhabitants.

A fantasy… of course. This is a place where human dramas have been played out on an operatic scale; where the destruction of the feudal clan system, following the Battle of Culloden in 1746, was rapidly succeeded by the infamous Highland Clearances that forced great shifts in the population, and added the motive of necessity to an already established enthusiasm for emigration. The Highlands today have modern industry and technology, a cultural life which is particularly rich in music and visual art and a population in which earlier influxes of Celts and Scandinavians have been joined by swathes of more recent immigrants, especially folk from the north of England who find the mountains and lochs and the wilder coastal places particularly congenial.

Yet, perhaps because it was considered a savage region until quite recent times and so stayed relatively isolated, or perhaps because the Gaelic language and its associated traditions still have a foothold, the Highlands, more than any other region of Britain, are rich with stories. The Scots word 'hoaching' would describe it better. Every peak and glen, every river, loch and pool, every track, forest and township, has an associated story. And these are tales not just written down in books, but known by communities and passed down through families: stories of fairies, ghosts, giants, waterhorses, witches, the second sight, feuds, betrayals, amorous deeds, and encounters with Old Nick himself.

A detour from the A9 at Newtonmore, along the B91512 and turning east for Coylumbridge just south of Aviemore, leads to Rothiemurchus, where some of the old Scots pines still stand. This is where our first story takes place.

# ～ The Flying Princess ～

Around 6,000 years ago, when the last remnants of ice from the last Ice Age had vanished from the most northerly parts of the Highlands, life, never completely absent, began to burgeon. Woodlands of juniper and birch started to spring up. Animals came: bear, wolf, beaver, reindeer, aurochs and more; and, of course, humans. Swathes of pine and oak established themselves further south, playing their part in the creation of the semi-mythical wildwood that became known as Caledon.

It wasn't long before people began to cut down the trees to make clearings where they could erect their dwellings; then to clear land to farm, and use the timber to fuel smelting and to build ships. Climate change, too, played a major part in deforestation, and by the eighteenth century little was left of the old wildwood. Stories began to be told about how and why the trees had disappeared. This is one of the oldest of those stories.

A long time ago, the King of Lochlann (which is the old name for the country we now call Norway), paid a state visit to Scotland. The King of Lochlann and the King of Scotland didn't get on. One reason was that the King of Lochlann was jealous of the Scottish forests, which were far finer than his own. He decided to act. He sent his daughter to the Isle of Skye, to learn the Black Arts. She was away for seven years, and when she returned home, she brought a little black book with her.

The Princess took the book and climbed to the highest room in the tallest tower of the castle. She locked the door behind her, opened the book, and began to read. As she read, a small cloud started to form outside the window of the highest room in the tallest tower; and as she continued to read, the cloud grew bigger.

When the Princess had finished her incantation, she closed the book and climbed up onto the window ledge. She leaned forward and slipped into the cloud, and the cloud, with a rumble, began to drift down towards the sea. As she flew through the air, the Princess sang a little song:

> Over the mountains, over the valleys
> Over the burns where salmon are leaping
> Down to the sea where sailors are calling
> Now my work has just begun

Across the sea flew the Princess, towards the north-east tip of Scotland – the place which today is called Caithness. When the cloud reached the coast, a bolt of lightning shot out of it, and struck the tops of the trees. Soon the great forest of birch and juniper was ablaze. The wall of fire advanced slowly southward, while behind it drifted the Princess in her cloud, singing softly. Ahead of the wall of fire ran the animals – wolves, bears, beavers, wild boar – and the people, the refugees, carrying what little they had managed to grab, before their homes were eaten by the flames. Up in her cloud, the Princess sang:

> Over the mountains, over the valleys
> Angel of death and fiery destruction
> People and creatures fleeing before me
> Now my work is almost done

When the first refugees reached Rothiemurchus, they told the people there what was happening. The folk of Rothiemurchus decided to go to the wise man for advice. They had a fine forest of pine trees and they didn't want to lose it.

'What shall we do?' they asked the wise man.

'The first thing, bring me all your silver,' he said.

They were poor people, and didn't have much, but they gathered together some coins, a couple of rings, a brooch and a bracelet, and took them to the wise man. He melted them down and made a silver arrowhead. He bound the arrowhead to a shaft made of rowan wood.

'What now?' asked the people. In the distance they could see the wall of flame, and the fire-breathing cloud getting closer and closer.

'Take all the mother animals. Take the sows and the mares, and the cows and the ewes, and herd them onto that hillside.'

They did this. 'What next?' they said.

'Take all the baby animals. Take the piglets and the foals, and the calves and the lambs, and put them on the hillside opposite.'

The people did this. The mothers saw the babies and the babies saw their mothers, far away on the opposite sides of the glen. They

let out such terrible, heartbreaking cries for each other, that the Princess popped her head out of the cloud to see what was making the racket.

The wise man drew back his bowstring and loosed the silver-tipped arrow. It flew through the air, and went straight into the Princess's heart. Out of the cloud she fell, and hit the ground, dead as a stone. The cloud became a mist and the mist evaporated. The wall of flame shrank to ashes.

And that's why, today, a little piece of the ancient Scottish pine forest is left in Rothiemurchus.

And that's also why, if you know the right place to go, you can still hear children in school playgrounds chanting this clapping rhyme:

A Princess came from over the sea
She came flying with a one, two, three
She flew 'til she came to the Caithness shore
She came flying with a two, three, four
She burnt all the trees and everything alive
She came flying with a three, four, five
She turned all the trees into little black sticks
She came flying with a four, five, six
All the animals cried to heaven
She came flying with a five, six, seven
They cried out early, they cried out late
She came flying with a six, seven, eight
Hear the silver arrow whine
She came flying with a seven, eight, nine
She'll never try her tricks again
Down she came with an eight, nine – TEN!

The road east from Rothiemurchus heads into the heart of the Cairngorm Mountains. At its end there's now a mountain railway that will take you to a restaurant near the top of Cairn Gorm – the Blue Mountain – itself. There are still stories told in this haven for skiers of the Big Grey Man, a presence who is seen, or sometimes just sensed, on the high places. But he's by no means the only giant in the Cairngorms. At the foot of the mountain is Glenmore, an easy and charming walk bordered by slopes of Scots pine to Lochan Uaine, the Green Lochan.

There are giants in the lands around Glenmore. Best known, perhaps, is Dòmhnull Mòr, Big Donald, the King of the Fairies. Lochan Uaine is green because Donald and his followers wash their clothes there, and fairies' clothes are green.

One evening, a certain Robin Òg Stewart of Kincardine was on his way home up the glen, when he heard the sound of pipes in the distance. He hid in the bushes and watched as Big Donald's fairy band approached. The pipes sounded so beautiful, and were so wonderfully decorated with silver trimmings, that Robin wanted a set for himself. So he stood up and shouted, 'Mine to you, yours to mine.' Then he threw his bonnet into the middle of the players, and grabbed some pipes.

The band carried on down the track, as if they hadn't noticed. Robin was well pleased with himself. He hid the pipes under his plaid and went on his way. But when he got back home, all he found in his hand was a puffball, with a twig sticking out of it.

The same Robin Òg was hunting in Glenmore one day, when he managed to bring down a magnificent hind. He started to gralloch the beast and for a moment put down his *sgian dubh* on the grass. When he looked for it, the knife had vanished; so he took out his dirk and carried on with the job. A minute later he put down the dirk, and it too vanished. Robin took the hind on his back and headed out of Glenmore as fast as he was able.

A while later he was on the shore of Loch Morlich, when he met an old man dressed in grey. The old man pointed at Robin, and Robin saw that his hand was dripping with blood.

'Now, Robin. You're here too often, killing my children. Remember that hind you slaughtered not so long ago? You can have your knives back, but don't let me see you in these parts again.'

Robin took the two knives from the old man, determined to change his hunting grounds. He realised that he was face to face with the Bodach Làmh Dheirg – the Old Man of the Bloody Hand. The Bodach was the guardian of the forest creatures. He more usually took the form of a gigantic warrior who challenged intruders in his domain to mortal combat. The brave, who immediately accepted, were spared, but the timorous met a dreadful end. Robin realised he'd had a very lucky escape.

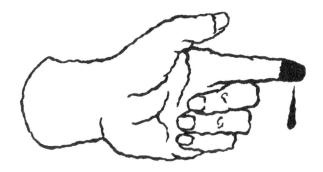

## ~ Margaret and the Three Gifts ~

Primarily it's the Victorians whom we have to thank for our notion that fairies are diminutive, winged creatures. In the Highlands, and in the Celtic countries in general, they are a quite different kind of being. A common belief is that the fairies – or the *daoine sìth*, the Good People – were fallen angels. When they were cast out of heaven, some fell in the sea, some on the land, and the rest took to the air. Those who fell on the land set up home in grassy mounds which are called *sìtheanan*, and the Highlands are full of these habitations. The *daoine sìth* lived, and still live, very close to us humans, and at certain times of the year the doors in the side of their homes are open, and we can peer inside – even enter. We should be cautious though, because tasting their food or drinking their wine – they are extremely hospitable folk – can put us in their thrall, and a happy evening in the Sìthean may turn out to have lasted many decades when we re-emerge into the human world.

The *daoine sìth* can be good neighbours, and can dally, even intermarry, with humans. But they can also steal from us, and they love to take away our babies.

Glenmore is the perfect setting for the story of Margaret, a young woman who was born with three gifts: a light hand for the baking; a light foot for the dancing; and a light heart to see her through the day.

Margaret lived in a cottage in a clearing in the Glen, with her husband Donald, and their little baby Angus; and if you asked Margaret which of the two – Donald or Angus – she loved the best, she would find it impossible to decide.

Donald was a drover, sometimes away for weeks at the markets in the south. One beautiful day in late summer, during one of his absences, Margaret decided to go on a picnic. She took a bottle of milk and some sandwiches, and set off with the baby up the track to the Green Lochan. In the early afternoon they stopped by a grassy knoll to rest. Margaret had unpacked the sandwiches and taken out the milk, when she noticed a cloud of dust coming up the track towards her. As the cloud got closer, she saw a little old man with a long white beard inside of it. He looked worn and weary, and the dust of the road was on him.

'Why don't you stop and share our picnic,' said Margaret. The little old man sat down beside her. He ate half the sandwiches and drank half the milk. Then he stood up, and spoke for the first time. 'You've been very kind to me. I have neither gold nor silver, but what I'm going to give you is more precious than either.'

He reached into his pocket, and pulled out a rusty old horseshoe nail. 'Take this,' he said, 'and look after it well. It may come in useful sooner than you think.'

Margaret was far too polite to ask what on earth she should be doing with a rusty old horseshoe nail. She thanked him, and slipped the nail into her apron pocket. The little old man set off back up the track, and soon he was gone from sight.

That evening it turned cold. Margaret placed baby Angus in his cot next to the fire, and put a sprig of rowan on top of his blanket, to keep him safe from evil spirits. As she sat spinning, she heard a terrible commotion out in the yard. She thought a fox must have got in among the chickens. She took the lantern and went out into the night to see what was happening, but there was no sign of any fox, and the chickens were safe in their coop.

Margaret went back into the house. As she closed the door, she heard a sound. Hehehehehe! She looked round the room, but couldn't see where the sound was coming from. Then she noticed that the sprig of rowan was lying on the floor. Margaret went over to the cot, and looked in. Where

baby Angus had lain, there was a skinny, brown, mottled thing, with long, sharp finger nails, pointed ears, big, yellow eyes, a grin that stretched from ear to ear, and a mouth full of sharp teeth. It looked up at her and laughed. Hehehehehe! Straightaway she knew what had happened. The fairies had tricked her into leaving the house. When she was outside, they'd stolen baby Angus and put one of their own in his place. A Changeling!

It took Margaret the whole of the night to decide what to do, and most of the next day to pluck up the courage to do it. When evening came she took the Changeling and wrapped it tightly in a blanket, so it couldn't scratch her face. Then she set off through the woods to the Sìthean, the fairy hill. It was dark when Margaret reached the Sìthean. She picked up a stone and hammered three times. A door opened in the side of the hill, on to a room filled with light. There, in the middle of the room, stood the Fairy Queen. She was a beautiful woman, but it was a cold beauty. By her side was a fairy servant and, in the servant's arms, baby Angus.

Margaret stepped inside the Sìthean. She dropped the Changeling on the floor and it scuttled away into a corner. 'I don't want that thing,' she said. 'I want my baby back.'

'I wonder what your baby's worth to you,' said the Fairy Queen. 'I hear you have a light hand for the baking. Would you give that in return for your baby?'

Margaret didn't have to think twice. She nodded. The Fairy Queen reached out and stroked her arm, and her hand became as heavy as lead.

'Now,' said Margaret, 'give me back my baby.'

'I didn't say I'd give him back.' said the Fairy Queen. 'I was just interested in what he was worth to you. Surely more than a light hand? I hear you have a light foot for the dancing. Would you give that in return for your baby?'

Again Margaret didn't have to think twice. She nodded. The Fairy Queen reached out and stroked her leg, and her foot became as heavy as lead.

'Now,' said Margaret, 'give me back my baby.'

'Did I say I'd give him back?' said the Fairy Queen. 'He must be worth more to you than a light hand and a light foot. I hear you have a light heart to see you through the day. Would you give that in return for your baby?'

This time Margaret did have to think. Without her light heart, she would always be gloomy, and it would be so hard to bring up a child in a house without joy. But she wanted Angus back so badly, that she nodded. The Fairy Queen reached out and stroked Margaret on the chest, and her heart went as heavy as lead.

'Now,' she said for a third time, 'give me back my baby.'

'Think,' said the Fairy Queen. 'If he comes back with you into the world of mortals, he'll grow old. Eventually he'll die. If he stays here in our world he'll always be young. Surely you'd like to give him immortality?'

Margaret lunged forward and grabbed Angus from the arms of the fairy servant. Then she turned and threw herself out of the mound into the darkness, and began to stumble through the trees. She thought that if she could reach the burn and get to the other side she would be safe, because the fairies can't cross running water. But she could feel them just behind her, playing with her hair, scratching her back with their long, sharp fingernails, and she knew that they could pounce at any time.

Then she tripped on a root and fell. The baby rolled out of her arms, and there was a chink. There was a chink as the rusty old horseshoe nail slipped out of her apron pocket and hit a stone. Margaret groped around and found the nail. She remembered that, if there's one thing the fairies hate more than running water, it's forged metal. She turned around, held up the nail, and made the sign of the cross.

'Stop!' said the Fairy Queen. 'Get back, get back. She has cold steel, she has cold steel!'

The fairies shrank back into the Sìthean, and the door slammed shut. At that moment, far away, a cockerel crew, and the sun began to rise. Margaret picked up Angus, and started off back home. As she went along the path she realised that, not only had she got her baby back, she'd got back her light hand and her light foot and her light heart.

# A GREAT GLEN
# GALLIMAUFRY

Inverness is the Highlands' only city, a compact place. The broad waters of the River Ness pass through it and flow away into the Moray Firth. There are mountains close by, but the land upon which the city itself is built slopes only gently. Tomnahurich Hill is a high point, rising dramatically by the side of the main road that heads west out of the city. Tomnahurich – which means 'the hill of the yews' – has been a cemetery since Victorian times. Long before that it was known to Invernesians as a Sìthean, a fairy mound. A well-known legend tells of two fiddle players who were up from Badenoch for a wedding. They were invited into Tomnahurich Hill, where there was a party going on, and their music helped greatly to make the celebrations go with a swing. The next morning, though, they found themselves out on the cold hillside in an Inverness that was quite unfamiliar. Because time inside the Sìthean passes more slowly than it does in the world of mortals, 100 years had gone by since the fiddlers entered the mound to spend their evening there. The two men wandered until they came to a church. As soon as they crossed the threshold, they crumbled into dust. A wind blew the dust away, and only their fiddles were left, abandoned on the ground.

Some time in the seventeenth century, Coinneach Odhar – Sallow Kenneth – predicted that, in the future, Tomnahurich Hill would be 'under lock and key, and the fairies secured within'. Kenneth Mackenzie is better known as the Brahan Seer, the legendary Highland Nostradamus, whose predictions were finally written down 200 years after they were purportedly made, when most had already been fulfilled. The seer also predicted the building of the Caledonian Canal, with the words, 'strange as it may seem to you this day, the time will come, and it is not far off, when full-rigged ships will be seen sailing eastward and westward, by the back of Tomnahurich near Inverness.'

The idea of linking up the natural waterways of the Great Glen – Loch Ness, Loch Oich, Loch Lochy and Loch Linnhe – in a continual passage from the Irish Channel to the North Sea had been mooted often in the latter part of the eighteenth century. When Thomas Telford was finally commissioned to do the work in 1803, Britain was at war with France and it was hoped that the canal would help to fulfil two aims: to provide a strategic advantage during the conflict, and to help stem emigration from the Highlands by providing employment. By the time work was complete, twelve years beyond the estimated date and massively over budget, the wars were over and depopulation was being driven even harder by the effects of the Highland Clearances, the piecemeal moving of communities from their homes to make way for more profitable sheep. The canal was too shallow for larger vessels, so its use for trade was limited, and it was twice closed in the 1840s so that improvements could be made. It settled down to become a route for fishing boats and tourism, with pleasure steamers plying the waters back and forth until the beginning of the Second World War.

The following handful of stories follows the route of the Great Glen and the Caledonian Canal, west from Inverness into the wilds of Lochaber. The first tale, though, happened long before the canal was even dreamed of.

# ~ The Golden Bowl ~

Loch Ness is, of course, the haunt of the famous and extremely elusive Loch Ness monster. The monster is only the best known among many similar creatures which inhabit the Highland lochs and the smaller stretches of water which are called lochans. They generally take the form of horses (though bulls are also spoken of) and are treacherous beasts. They lure unsuspecting innocents – often young girls or children – to mount them, and then plunge into their watery homes to drown their victims, of whom no trace, apart from a liver or occasionally a heart, will ever be found. An *each uisge* – waterhorse – was reported in the 1850s 'basking on the surface' of Loch Arkaig. The witness 'only saw the head and hind quarters, proving that its back was hollow, which is not the shape of any fish or of a seal. Its head resembled that of a horse'.

The first sighting of the monster of Loch Ness is much earlier, for, in the sixth century, St Columba subdued it after it had killed a man. It makes a brief appearance in this story about King Brude of the Picts, who was a contemporary of Columba.

When Brude grew to be an old man he spent more and more time in the fortress at the east end of the deep, wide stretch of water we now call Loch Ness. He had fought many battles, and won most of them. He enjoyed good food, music and singing, though storytellers tended to bore him with their constant harping on about giants and princesses. One thing that particularly pleased him, though he couldn't be sure why, was the friendship he had formed with Colum, the Irishman from the west. Brude wasn't much interested in religion. When Colum first arrived and tried to convert everyone to the idea of a god who was also a man, and who seemed to have come to a very sticky end, the king gave him short shrift. However, when they got to know each other a little better, they got on famously. Both enjoyed a drink, and both were warriors with warriors' hearts.

What endeared Colum to Brude more than anything else, though, was the way the Irishman had dealt with Brude's own priests. These priests were a small band of elderly men who had cultivated their hair – what they had of it – and their beards to a great length, and who seemed to be present at every recurring quotidian and annual event, as if, without their intervention, life wouldn't proceed just as it had for millennia. When the sun rose and when it set, at the full moon and the new, when seed was planted and when the crops were harvested, at the bonfires of mid-summer and the bonfires of mid-winter, when battles commenced and while the dead were being buried, at births and deaths, and even at the consummation of royal marriages, they were there with their mutterings, their invocations and their inscrutable ceremonies. Brude thought them no more than a bunch of second-rate conjurers. He would have kicked them out years before, had it not been that his wife, a red-haired beauty who was quite a bit younger than him, had a great enthusiasm for anything that involved incantations, potions, horoscopes or communicating with the spirit world. So the king was secretly delighted when Colum had proved himself by far the greater magician, cursing and then curing Brude's chief priest, sending packing the troublesome waterhorse that terrorised swimmers in the loch, and conquering a storm that the Pictish priests claimed to have whipped up in a vain attempt to hamper his return to the west.

Since then, Colum had made a couple more visits up the water in his skin-covered boat. After supper he and Brude would stroll round the ramparts of the fort, sharing stories of battles – battles of blood and bone, and battles of the soul. But the last time they were together, Brude noticed how frail his old friend looked, and secretly feared that this would be their last meeting on Earth, though perhaps not the very last meeting, if Colum's crazy ideas about a heaven proved to be right after all.

So there was Brude, the old king dreaming in his fort. He was content that he had achieved a kind of peace for his realm and more than content with his wife, who was still a very beautiful woman, even if the fire of her hair was a little dimmed these days. But there were two things that pleased Brude more than anything else in this world. The first was to go hunting. Colum, late at night by the fire, used to tell stories of a great Irish warrior chief called Finn. This man's deeds were extraordinary, and Brude doubted the truth of the tales. But, like him, Finn was a hunter, so he felt an affinity for the fellow. Finn's favourite dog was called Bran and when, after what would indeed prove to be Colum's final visit, a fine bitch of

Brude's had given birth to pups, the king named the firstborn Bran, in memory of his old friend. Bran had proved to be a great dog; he could pull down a stag or rip the throat out of a wolf fearlessly and without help. Now, like his master, he was old and grey, but the two of them would still go out together, enjoying each other's company and often managing to catch a squirrel or even an elderly hare.

The second thing that pleased Brude was to receive presents. Word of this love of gifts had spread. Every morning, before dawn, a small crowd gathered at the gates of the fort, people who bore something they were sure would delight the king. Some came because they revered the old man and wanted to please him. Some thought their gifts might curry favour. Others, mostly young people, had travelled a good distance, and looked upon the enterprise primarily as an adventure.

In truth, the king was more affected by the act of giving than by the gift itself. Each morning there were servants waiting at the gate to receive the presents, which they then took and placed in a massive storehouse that the king had had specially built. Once a week Brude would visit the storehouse and wander among the shelves, among the portraits which showed him victorious over enemies, the commemorative medallions, and the carved inscriptions in wood and stone extolling his virtues. He seldom paused to examine any single gift but, on this particular morning, something caught his attention. It was a small, perfectly square box, made out of a fine-grained, light-coloured wood, and no joints were visible in its construction. Brude took the box off the shelf. He lifted the lid. Inside, fitting snugly, was a golden bowl. The old king slipped the bowl out of the box and turned it around in his hand. Within the rim there was writing, in Ogham script. It said: GIVE THIS BOWL TO THE ONE YOU LOVE MOST.

The queen sat in her chamber with a mirror in one hand and an exquisite bone comb in the other, dragging the comb through her long, red hair. There was a knock at the door. 'Come in,' she said, without looking round.

'I've something for you.' She saw, behind her, her husband reflected in the mirror.

'How sweet,' she said. 'Thank you, darling, what a lovely man you are. Just put it on the table by my bed. I'll look at it as soon as I've finished my toilette.' When the combing was done, the queen stood and noticed something glittering on the bedside table. It was

a golden bowl. She picked it up and turned it around in her hand. There was writing inside the rim. It said: GIVE THIS BOWL TO THE ONE YOU LOVE THE MOST.

The queen put on her robe and slipped the bowl into her sleeve. She went out of the palace and crossed the courtyard to the barracks, making sure no one saw her. Once in the barracks she went down to the far end of the corridor and into the last room, where the handsome young Captain of the Guard was putting on his uniform. The queen embraced the Captain of the Guard, kissed him, and said, 'I've a present for you. Something special.' She took the bowl from her sleeve and pressed it into his hands.

'Thank you,' said the Captain of the Guard. 'That's wonderful.'

The queen kissed him again. 'I have to go now, but we'll meet soon.' Then she left the barracks as secretly as she came.

When the queen was gone, the Captain of the Guard picked up the golden bowl, and saw that inside the rim was written: GIVE THIS BOWL TO THE ONE YOU LOVE THE MOST. He went into the little side room where his fourteen-year-old son was asleep, and set the bowl down on the floor at the side of the boy's bed. Then he went out onto the parade ground.

The Captain of the Guard's son woke some time after noon. He opened his eyes and saw a golden bowl, glistening in a beam of sunlight from the high, narrow window. He sat up and took the bowl, and turned it around in his hands, and he saw that on the inside of the rim were the words: GIVE THIS BOWL TO THE ONE YOU LOVE THE MOST.

The boy sprang out of bed. He pulled on his clothes, sprinted out of the barracks and across the courtyard, and dived down the steps into the kitchens. The pretty little servant girl who did all the menial tasks was sweeping the floor. The Captain of the Guard's son skidded to a halt in front of her, and held out the golden bowl. 'This is for you.'

The little servant girl stared saucer-eyed at the bowl. 'It's beautiful,' she said. 'Thank you. As soon as I've finished work I'll really look at it.' And she slid the bowl into her apron pocket. The boy was already out of the kitchens.

After she had finished sweeping the floor, had fetched water, chopped vegetables and cleared out the ashes from the hearth, the little servant girl was told she could take a break until it was time to start cooking the evening meal. Out in the courtyard she took the bowl from her apron pocket and turned it around in her hands. She saw that there was something written inside the rim, but she had no idea what it said, because she couldn't read.

One of the priests was walking close by the kitchens. Like his fellows he wore a stern expression, and his long and luxuriant beard gave him a particularly forbidding aspect; but in the past he had spoken some kind words to the little servant girl, so she gathered her courage, stepped out in front of him, and held up the bowl.

'What's this?' said the old man. The little servant girl didn't say anything, so the priest took the bowl from her, and turned it around in his hands. 'This is a very precious thing. Do you know what this writing says?' The little servant girl shook her head. 'Whoever gave this to you must think very highly of you, because it says "give this bowl to the one you love the most". You should take great care of it.'

The priest gave back the bowl and went on his way. The little servant girl crossed the courtyard to the magnificent wooden building where the king had his quarters. She slipped past the guard, who was dozing in the afternoon sun, and went in.

King Brude was in his room. He was a little bored, and wondering what to do for the rest of the day, when there was a knock at the door. The king went to see who it was. The servant girl from the kitchens stood there. A pretty little thing, she had come to the fort as a slave and he had granted her freedom. He always made a point of having a few words with her whenever their paths crossed. She held up to him something small and shiny, which he took from her. Then, without speaking, she ran down the corridor and out of the building.

Brude turned the small, shiny thing round in his hands. It was a golden bowl, a familiar golden bowl, and on the inside of the rim was written, in Ogham script: GIVE THIS BOWL TO THE ONE YOU LOVE THE MOST. He took the pitcher from the wash stand, poured water into the bowl and set it down on the stone floor. His old hunting dog heard the chink and raised its head. It stood, slowly came over, and began to drink.

When all the water was drained from the bowl, King Brude took his walking staff from behind the door. 'Come on, Bran,' he said to the dog. 'Let's go hunting.'

## ⁓ Angie and the Calf ⁓

The main road out of Inverness to the west is the A82, which runs along the north side of Loch Ness. The narrow, winding A82 has its charms – caravans, camper vans and heavy goods vehicles are not among them – but the network of minor roads on the south side of the loch passes through a much more varied landscape and is less fraught with frustration for a driver who is planning a leisurely trip to Fort Augustus.

The late Hugh MacNally lived in Gorthleck on this south side of the loch. He was a scholar, a composer of celebratory tunes, a melodeon player, and one of the most invigorating players of the harmonica I have heard. He was also a charming storyteller with a gentle sense of humour. The story of Angie and the Calf is given in his own words.

This is the story of a well-known and much loved character from Stratherrick, on the south side of Loch Ness; a young man known as Angie Ruadh (red-haired Angus). He was brought up on a small croft and, by the time Angie was in his late teens, his father was getting rather old and a bit frail, so that more and more work, and more responsibility, was devolving to Angus. In these days, responsibility was something that the old folks hung on to for a very long time. One of the major incomes for the small croft at that time was the annual calf sale. They only had one cow and there was only ever one calf. But the proceeds from that calf could pay the rent, or buy the meal or whatever; it was a very necessary part of their livelihood, and, of course, the father was in the habit, each year, of taking the calf to Inverness to sell it.

He'd now reached the stage where he was getting pretty sore and infirm, and he thought it was time that Angie could take the calf on his behalf. Angie was more than delighted, but it involved carrying a calf 5 miles, nearly 6 miles, to Inverfarigaig pier. It would either be carried in a bag or placed in a wheelbarrow that they trundled down to the pier, and there they would pick up the boat which plied the route from Fort Augustus to Inverness daily. And where

it came into the terminal at Inverness, it was at the Tomnahurich Bridge, and from there on, there was stagecoach and haulage transport to the middle of town for the like of the farmers en route to the sale yard.

So Angie duly set off with the calf on this particular occasion and had no problems – he reached Inverness, and he reached the sale yard and he sold the calf. Its value would only be counted in shillings in those days, because we're talking about 100 years ago. Angie then had time on his hands before he had to do the return journey.

We don't know what transpired in the town, but he would have met a lot of old friends and some neighbours; it was a time of semi-celebration in a way. If there was any celebration in the town then that was bad enough, but when you got back to the boat… the boat, of course, was even better equipped than the town, because there was a residents' bar and there was nothing else to do but pass the time. You can imagine – because Angie was jingling money in his pocket, and he was quite the big man – his friends and neighbours would be congratulating him on getting good money for the calf, and asking how was the family, and generally flattering him, and one thing led to another. And one would stand a round and the next fellow would stand a round, and this went on, and by the time the boat reached Inverfarigaig again Angie was in great form, but his pockets were just about empty. And he had to set out for home.

You can imagine after 5 miles of walking he'd be pretty sober and we don't know what thoughts were in his mind, but the moment of truth was when the old man asked how he had got on and put his hands out for the cash.

The cash wasn't there. There were only a few pennies in his pocket. It was pretty devastating. Nobody knows what was said, but Angie on the whole was pretty satisfied it was worth it. Nobody beat him over the head with a stick or anything, and he thought, well, time heals all wounds. And the old folks, of course they were upset, but time went on and time went on. Another year had passed, another calf had been produced, and it was time for the calf to be disposed of. Angie by this time thought it was almost forgotten, and he was looking forward to a repeat, or at least another good outing.

But the days were passing and the weeks were passing, and the calf was getting bigger. Angie of course wasn't going to say a word, and the father was determined he wasn't going to say a word either. This went on, and at last Angie had to give in, and one morning he said to his father, 'When are we putting the calf away Father?'

'We're not!'

'But what will you do with it, Father?'

'We'll eat it. You drank the last one.'

# ⁓ Big Sandy of the Goblin ⁓

Many eccentric and flamboyant characters have made their homes along the Great Glen waterway. Visitors to Fort Augustus in the latter half of the nineteenth century could visit the collection of hunting trophies of Roualeyn George Gordon-Cumming, known as 'The Lion Hunter', who had retired there after a spectacular career as an adventurer in Africa. Another who frequented the Great Glen in more recent times was Steanie the Warlock. He hawked copies of his verses which, I've been told, were printed for him by the monks of Fort Augustus Abbey as an act of charity. Steanie was one of the band of itinerants – 'trampie men' – who stravaiged through the Highlands between the two great wars of the twentieth century. Forty Pockets was another, a well-kent figure on the streets of Inverness. A black and white photo shows him, perhaps performing a little dance, wearing the famous coat of forty pockets.

More recently still, the great Highland fiddle player Angus Grant, who was brought up in Fort Augustus, remembers Jimmy the Dolphin:

> He was a bit of a religious fanatic, and he'd charge down the village now and again shouting, 'Christ walked on the water, and he'll let me walk on the water', and he'd just run right onto the canal. And of course all the lock keepers heard him coming, and they were waiting there with boat hooks. Jimmy would disappear, and they'd pull him up and say, 'Let you down again, Jimmy!'

Towards the end of the eighteenth century a man called Sandy McDonell worked on the Invergarry estate, just south of Fort Augustus. He was known to everyone as Alasdair Mòr a'Bhòchdain – Big Sandy of the Goblin – and he was celebrated not just for his physical strength, but as a raconteur and for his skill in predicting the future.

This is how Sandy got his name and his gifts as a seer.

On winter nights Sandy was a frequent visitor to Invergarry House, where he would entertain the company with stories of his great strength. One night when there was a full moon in the sky, he was on his way back up the glen to his home at Munerigie. A big dog crossed the road in front of him. Sandy imagined that one of Glengarry's deerhounds had slipped out and followed him. He cursed the dog, and ordered it to go straight back home. The dog immediately took on human form and, in Gaelic, challenged him to a fight; so Sandy and the goblin set to. This was the first of many such contests, which often lasted until dawn, when the goblin would flee at first light; as such creatures tend to do.

Between rounds, the goblin and Sandy would chat, and the goblin would pass on information about future events. Sandy in turn relayed these predictions to his friends, though they seemed so outlandish that no one believed him. One pronouncement in particular got him into trouble, which was that the House of Glengarry would soon collapse. When word of this reached Glengarry, Sandy was summoned to Invergarry House to account for himself. He confirmed the truth of his prediction and was promptly thrown out, but its accuracy eventually established his reputation as a seer, for within twenty-five years the chief was dead, and his son was forced to sell the estates.

The battles between Sandy and the goblin continued. The goblin would appear whenever the urge took its fancy, sometimes at the most inconvenient times; so, for example, Sandy might be at a dance when he was called on to fight. He would stop mid-step and march out of the hall, while the musicians and the other dancers stopped as well, and everyone crowded at the window to watch Sandy out there in the twilight, falling back, springing up, pummelling thin air – for no one but he could see the demonic opponent.

Early in the nineteenth century, Sandy found himself in the Black Watch, fighting in the Peninsular War. The goblin was at his side, keeping an eye on him and assuring him that he would get back home safely. Following the fall of San Sebastián many British officers had been killed, and wild behaviour broke out among the troops. Rambling through the streets, Sandy saw a group of soldiers in an upstairs room enjoying a keg of brandy, and thought he would join them. When he reached the top of the stairs, one of them, who he had never seen before, gave him a thump in the

stomach that doubled him up; another blow knocked him back
down the stairs to the ground floor. The other soldiers asked the
assailant, who was a Mackay from Sutherland, what on earth he
was up to. He replied that he had heard that his victim was the
strongest man in all the Scottish regiments, and had wanted to try
him out.

Eventually, as the goblin had promised, Sandy got back home
safely to Munerigie. The spectral assaults continued, and finally
Sandy grew so sick of them that he decided to emigrate to America.
After calling at the various ports to pick up other passengers, and
enduring a long, stormy crossing, they reached Boston. The goblin
was waiting for Sandy on the quay.

'Hey Sandy, how are you faring?'

'I'm faring badly. That was a hard crossing.'

'How long did it take you?'

'Six months. How long did it take you?'

'Oh I set off just this afternoon.'

Sandy realised he would never shake off the goblin. He was getting on in years and, rather than face a new life in a strange country, he decided to return to Munerigie. The veterans of the war against Bonaparte went periodically to Fort Augustus to collect their pensions, and after they received payment they would gather in an inn to enjoy a dram. On one of these occasions, a man who was sitting in a corner of the room got up and came over to Sandy.

'Do you remember seeing me in San Sebastián?'

Sandy shook his head.

'Do you remember a soldier knocking you down the stairs?'

Indeed, Sandy did remember.

'Well, that was me.'

It was a reunion of sorts, and the two had a glass together for the sake of old times. The rest of the veterans decided that the earlier bout in San Sebastián was no kind of competition at all, and that Mackay and McDonell should fight again in Fort Augustus. The two arm-wrestled for an hour. There was no clear winner, but the company agreed that if Sandy had been younger he would certainly have gained the upper hand.

Year after year, the goblin returned to pick fights with Sandy. As Sandy got older this became more and more wearying. One day they were tussling and the goblin had Sandy crouched down on one knee. 'God bless me,' said Sandy, 'I'm getting too old for this.'

The goblin stood back. 'If you'd said that to me when we started this business all those years ago, I would never have bothered you.'

All it had needed was that simple prayer. The goblin swirled away in a mist, and that was the last Sandy, or any other mortal, saw of it.

Kildonan graveyard is just by the side of the A87, close to Munerigie. It's a peaceful spot, and slightly mysterious, for many of the older stones have no inscription, and are so roughly hewn that they look as if they could have been retrieved from a Neolithic cemetery. In the middle of the burial ground is a huge, long stone laid flat on the ground. It's said that this is Sandy's grave, and that he brought the stone here himself, on his back, in anticipation of his end. Close by is a stream which is still known as Caochan Glac a'Bhòchdain – the Burn of the Glade of the Goblin.

## — The Three Red Hats —

Continuing west along the A87 will bring you to Kintail. There, on the shores of Loch Duich, lived a young fisherman called Ruairidh. This was in the early 1970s, and Ruairidh was what used to be called a drop-out. After leaving school he'd tried a few jobs, working in the town and on various estates, but nothing really suited him. So he'd decided to set up on his own as a fisherman, while his wife, Marie, displayed her handmade cards and woven wall-hangings in a little gallery that tourists visited from time to time.

Ruairidh, however, wasn't much of a fisherman. His foremost pleasure was to play the guitar, an old Gibson Kalamazoo acoustic, which, together with a copy of *Be Here Now* by Baba Ram Dass, was, apart from Marie and his children, his most precious possession. Often, when he should have been out in the boat, Ruairidh would be sitting on the porch overlooking the loch, picking on the guitar. When Marie sensibly pointed out that they and the three children had to eat, he would reluctantly go out on the water – but would often take the Gibson along for company.

One evening, in late October, there was a terrible storm. The children slept through it, but Ruairidh and Marie were kept awake all night as the wind and rain crashed and blundered round their cottage. The next morning was bright and still. Encouraged by Marie, Ruairidh set off with his guitar to go fishing, but when he reached the loch shore he found his boat submerged in the shallows. During the storm it had been dashed against a rock, and there was a panel missing from its side. Ruairidh wandered up and down the shore, hoping to find the panel, but there was no sign of it, so he went back to the cottage and told Marie what had happened.

'Maybe best,' he said, 'if I get a lift into town next week and get some wood there.' Marie sent him straight back out again, telling him there was a forest at the back of the cottage that was full of wood, and not to come back until he'd found a piece that would fix the boat.

Ruairidh made himself a couple of sandwiches and set off into the forest. It was a fascinating place in the autumn, full of richly coloured, strangely shaped fungi that Ruairidh paused again and again to examine. Hardly an hour seemed to have passed before he became aware that the light was going. He looked around and there was no trace of the path. The best place to get an idea of where I am, thought Ruairidh, is from the top of one of these trees, so he shinned up an old Granny pine, right to the top, and sat in the branches. Then he opened his sandwiches and looked out over the forest. From up there things looked so different. The forest extended to the horizon in every direction. The treetops were dark and still because the sun had just gone down, leaving behind a clear, deep blue sky with one star burning brightly. Or maybe, thought Ruairidh, it's a planet.

A sound came drifting through from far off in the forest, an unusual howling which must have been made by a stray dog, though it did make Ruairidh shiver a little. Who knew what might be out in those woods, for there were stories of people living in the Highlands who bred savage animals in secret and then released them into the wilderness just to see how they would fare. He was thinking it would perhaps be safest to spend the night in the top of the Granny pine, when his eye was taken by what looked like a curl of smoke rising above the trees not so far away. Where there's smoke there's fire, he thought, and where there's fire there are people.

Back down on the forest floor, Ruairidh began to make his way towards the column of smoke. He heard the howling again, maybe a little closer, and hurried on, and soon he came to a clearing. In the middle of the clearing was a small stone house with a thatched roof, and out of a hole in the thatch came the smoke.

Ruairidh went up to the door, knocked and waited. The door opened and a tiny old woman stood looking up at him, with a face as wrinkled as an apple that's been kept all winter at the bottom of a barrel. She beckoned him over the threshold, and led him into a room where, on either side of a peat fire, sat two more tiny old women, both with those wrinkled apple faces. The first old woman pointed to a big wooden chair, and Ruairidh took it that he was to sit. There was a pot of something bubbling over the fire. The old woman scooped some of the contents into a bowl and handed it to Ruairidh. It was the best stew he had ever tasted, rabbit he reckoned. When the bowl was scraped clean the old woman went to a cupboard, poured something into a wooden vessel and passed it to him, and he sipped what must have been a dram, but whisky like he'd never tasted before, and a powerful distillation.

Someone prodded him gently in the shoulder. He must have dropped off for a moment. The old woman took an oil lamp and led him by the sleeve, along a corridor and into another room, which was empty but for a large bed and a kist by the window; she nodded to the bed, and left the room. Ruairidh sat on the edge of the bed, kicked off his shoes and dropped his jacket on the floor, lay down and went straight to sleep. Later in the night he woke suddenly, and he wasn't sure why. The room was now full of moonlight. Lying on the bed, quite still and with his eyes wide open, Ruairidh watched as one of the tiny old women crossed the room and made for the kist by the window. She lifted the lid and took out a little red cap, then put the cap on her head, clapped her hands, and said, 'Awa' tae London!' and she disappeared up the chimney with a Whoosh.

After a couple of minutes Ruairidh wasn't sure whether he'd seen the old woman vanish or just dreamed it, and he was soon asleep again; but not long after, he woke and watched a second old lady open the kist, take out a red cap and put it on her head, clap her hands and say, 'Awa' tae London!' and disappear with a Whoosh. And he didn't have time to fall asleep before the whole rigmarole unravelled a third time, and the last tiny old woman went up the chimney. Ruairidh climbed off the bed and crossed barefoot to the window. He lifted the lid of the kist. There was nothing inside but a little red cap, so he put the cap on his head and said, 'Awa' tae London!'

It was a pub like none that Ruairidh had seen before, a wild place. Drink was being served straight from barrels and out of unmarked bottles. Everyone was in fancy dress, as if they were part of a television costume drama. Fights broke out and were quickly quelled, and a handsome girl was dancing to the music of a fiddler. Across the table sat the three tiny old women, plainly in their cups and having the time of their lives. Another handsome girl placed a tray full of drinks between them, and Ruairidh leaned forward to take his share. What with exhaustion from the previous day's travails and the great quantities of drink he had consumed, he hardly noticed as each tiny old lady in turn donned a red cap, clapped her hands, said, 'Awa' hame,' and disappeared from the table in a puff of smoke.

A sharp finger jabbed his ribs. Ruairidh opened his eyes. The dancing girl, the fiddler, the drinkers and the brawlers, the tiny old ladies, all had gone. He was left among the debris of the previous night's fun with no shoes, no jacket, no money, and a big bill to foot for the festivities; a typical vagrant. It was when he was taken before a judge and condemned to be hanged for what seemed such a minor crime, that Ruairidh began to think he must be in a foreign country and in different times. All night he was kept awake by the hammering together of the scaffold outside in the street, and at first light his hands were bound behind him, and he was taken out to meet his end. The hangman slipped the noose over his head, and asked whether he had any last requests.

'There's just one thing,' said Ruairidh, whose wits had been considerably sharpened by the experiences of the last couple of days. 'My granny used to love to knit for me, and there's something she made that I always keep with me. It's a little red cap, and it's in my back pocket. If you could just put it on my head I know Granny would be happy that I'd died wearing it.'

The hangman took the hat out of Ruairidh's back pocket and did as he had requested. Ruairidh, with his hands tied behind his back, clapped them as best as he was able. He was taken up as if by a whirlwind, through dark, roaring spaces, and deposited in early morning sunlight on the shore of Loch Duich. The rope was still round his neck, and on the end of the rope the cross piece of the gallows. Close by in the water Ruairidh's boat lay half-submerged, and, as he looked at it, he realised that the cross piece was exactly the right size to repair the hole which had been the cause of all his adventures.

Back to the Great Glen, and the banks of the Caledonian Canal, which were once dotted with itinerant entertainers in the places where boats had to pause. Pipers were common, and there was one character who was always at Laggan locks, at the east end of Loch Lochy, the highest point of the canal, 106ft above sea level. He was known as 'Paddy'. He wore a black jacket, a white shirt, a bow tie, white breeches, black stockings and buckled shoes. Paddy must have been a popular character, for he appears on a postcard, jacket slung back off one shoulder, hat jauntily pulled down over his left eye, and looking as if he has just stepped off the music hall stage. A photograph from 1898 shows him together with a young boy, who seems to be dancing and playing a flute at the same time. At the end of the canal season Paddy used to tour through the Highland villages.

What Paddy himself did to entertain is unclear, but he must have kept up his annual perambulations well into the 1920s, because Dolly MacDonald remembers him coming to the Seaboard villages on the Nigg peninsula – over 80 miles' distance from Laggan – when she was a girl. He was something of an enigma, for no one knew where he slept at night, and his costume always seemed to be spotlessly clean.

Today it's easy to traverse the Great Glen. The road round the lochs may not be the straightest or the fastest, but by car the journey from sea to sea shouldn't normally take more than three hours. To commemorate the opening of the Caledonian Canal, the Poet Laureate, Robert Southey, spoke of Telford and his navvies 'opening a passage through the wilds subdued'.

In the days when this was still a wild place, at the opposite end of Loch Lochy from Laggan – where Paddy once performed – in a place called Moy, there lived another mysterious and travelled being. Her name was Gormshuil – the Blue-Eyed One – and she had, on one occasion, been summoned as far away as the island of Mull to help her sisters-in-sorcery rid Tobermory harbour of a Spanish galleon.

At a time when England was at war with Spain, the ship had been driven into the harbour by bad weather. The Tobermory people didn't want it there, so they called on An Dòideag Mhuileach, the famous Mull Witch, to use her powers to destroy it. To help her, she called on her two sisters, Ladhrig Thiristeach – the Hoofed One of Tiree – and the Islay Hag, a'Ghlaisrig Ìleach. Between them they invoked a storm that ripped up trees by the roots and tore the thatch off the houses; but the harbour was such a safe haven that the water there stayed as smooth as glass.

The witches agreed to call on Gormshuil of Moy. 'If she can't help, no one can.' The Blue-Eyed One gathered together all the cats on Mull, and many cats from other places too, and set them down on the deck of the galleon. It didn't take long for them to eat up the whole of the crew, and maybe nibble a few holes in the hull as well, because the galleon went down, and still lies at the bottom of Tobermory harbour, together with its treasure of gold doubloons.

Moy is in Cameron country, and Gormshuil was a Cameron who had married a Mackinnon. It's sometimes said that she had only one blue eye and that it was in the middle of her forehead, but this is just folklore. She was a vibrant, sharp-witted young woman, and was happy to be credited with magical powers and the second sight, because this made people slightly afraid of her; and, in her day, when the Highlands were riven by rivalry and factions, this could be a great advantage for an individual. People used to say of her, 'There's more to her than just telling the rosary beads', which was their way of expressing the awe in which she was held. When fishermen set out to catch salmon, or hunters went to the hill, they would always come to her to ask a blessing.

One day Lochiel, the clan chieftain of the Camerons, was on his way to meet the Duke of Atholl. They were to discuss the boundaries between their lands, and Atholl had suggested that they meet accompanied only by their pipers. On his way to the meeting, Lochiel passed by Gormshuil's house. The Blue-Eyed One sat in her doorway, singing softly to herself. As Lochiel rode by she called out to him, and asked where he was going.

'What's it to you?' Lochiel shot back, taken aback by her familiarity.

'Fishermen and hunters do well enough by my blessing. Who would I give it more willingly to than my chief?'

So Lochiel told Gormshuil that he was off to discuss boundaries with Atholl, taking only his piper with him. She told him to return home and gather together some of his men. When they got close to the meeting place, the men should hide in the heather, and Lochiel go forward with just his piper, as Atholl expected. If Lochiel opened his coat to show the scarlet lining, that would be a signal for his men to rush forward to his aid.

Lochiel did as Gormshuil had suggested. He met the Earl of Atholl at the appointed place, and they began to argue. The Earl demanded a bigger portion of land than he was due, and, when they couldn't agree, he took a silver whistle from his pocket and blew a shrill, piercing note. A dozen or so armed men sprang up from their hiding places among the bushes and heather.

'Who are these?' demanded Lochiel.

'These are the Atholl sheep, come to eat the Lochaber grass.'

Lochiel turned, and flung his coat wide to show the scarlet lining. His supporters rose up to confront Atholl's men.

'And these,' said Lochiel, 'are the Lochaber dogs, come to drive off the Atholl sheep.' Lochiel's piper began to play in triumph as the Atholl sheep trotted away across the moor.

On his return journey, Lochiel called at Gormshuil's house to thank her for her good advice. He told her to call on him any time she needed a favour in return. She replied that she was glad he had managed to get the better of the Duke of Atholl. 'Nevertheless,' she said, 'although you mean well with your promises, one day you will hang my son.'

Lochiel assured her that this would never be the case. 'Just come to me. Even if your son deserved to hang, I would save him for your sake.'

Time passed, and Gormshuil's son grew to be a young man. One day he was out on the hill with the son of a neighbour. A man passed by with whom they had some kind of quarrel. A fight broke out and the neighbour's son landed a blow that killed the man, though he had no intention of doing so. He was an only child, and his mother went to the Blue-Eyed One, terrified that her son would be executed for the crime. Gormshuil remembered Lochiel's promise, and got her own son to take the blame for the murder. He was imprisoned in a dungeon with an iron door, which looked out on Loch Arkaig.

Gormshuil set off for Achnacarry to plead for her son's life. On the way she came to a pool in a burn, and in the pool was a fat salmon. She thought it would be easy to catch with a little help, and called on some passers-by to assist, but they shunned her and hurried on along the road. Gormshuil went into the pool by herself, and knelt down. Very slowly she stretched out her hands towards the fish and, at that moment, the spate rushed down the stream and swept her into Loch Lochy, where she drowned.

Her son was hanged for a crime he didn't commit, just as his mother had foretold.

# BOGLES,
# BIG FELLOWS
# AND A BLACKSMITH

The A832 leaves the Inverness to Ullapool Road just after Garve, which was once a notorious haunt of highwaymen, and the place where Big Hughie Kilpatrick had a bloody encounter with the buck goat. It heads west through Strath Bran – perhaps named for the favourite dog of Finn MacCool, the mythical Irish warrior – and runs alongside the famous Kyle of Lochalsh railway line. At Achnasheen, the traveller can scale the heights of Glen Docherty for a spectacular view of Loch Maree, or head south-west towards Lochcarron, along stretches of winding single-track road, among steep passes wooded with Scots pine, into yet more mountainous terrain.

A couple of miles before Lochcarron is the Smithy, once a working forge and now a heritage centre. One November evening in 2003, Duncan Williamson visited here, when he was taking part in the annual Tales at Martinmas storytelling festival. Duncan was one of the most renowned storytellers of the twentieth century. He was born by the shores of Loch Fyne in Argyll in 1928, in a tent in a woodland clearing. In his autobiography, *The Horsieman*, he says that he was the seventh of the sixteen children of John Williamson and Betsy Townsley, who were both Travellers. During the summer months the family would go on the road, hawking and living off the land, and from autumn to spring the children went to Furnace Village School. Later in life, Duncan was an enthusiastic advocate of the Jew's harp, and his performances would inevitably include a piece on that subtle and seductive instrument. He often told the story of how he was taught to play by Miss MacFarlane, the head teacher of Furnace School, who passed on the technique in return for Duncan learning his alphabet, the ABC.

There was another, rather sad, tale from those days which reflects Duncan's early love of stories. A highlight of the Williamson children's lives was when they were able to spend time with their granny, Betsy's mother, because she was a great storyteller. She had a little bag, done up with three mother of pearl buttons, which contained her personal possessions, and she told the children that she also kept her stories there. One day, when she was asleep, Duncan and his sister sneaked a look in the bag. They found all manner of interesting things, but no stories. Later, the children asked Granny to tell them a tale. The old woman looked in her bag and declared that someone had been prying, and all the tales were gone; and she never again told them a single story.

Duncan died in 2007. In many ways he had a very fortunate life. He left the family tent when he was fourteen, and travelled widely in Argyll, Fife, Angus and the north-east, learning whatever trades were necessary to make a living, including how to handle horses; and he picked up songs and stories wherever he went. After his first wife died, he met Linda Headlee, a young American folklore student. They married, and lived together in Duncan's tent, where Linda bore their two children. She recognised both his importance as a bearer of traditional lore and his skills as a passionate communicator of that lore. She was able to get the books of his stories published, which led to his widespread recognition and invitations to travel the world to practise his art.

Towards the end of his life, Duncan spent time in a rented farm cottage near Collessie in Fife. He kept an open house. Visitors were welcomed into a small, dark living room where, whatever the weather, a fire would be blazing in the hearth: a focal point, like the fire on a Travellers' campsite. The host would ask, as a host should, after the well-being of the guests, of their next of kin, and of mutual friends. Somewhere in the background would be flitting a young person, probably a student come to research the life and skills of the great storyteller but, on this occasion at least, an all-important maker of tea. Suddenly, as if a switch had been thrown, a quizzical expression would come over Duncan's puckish face, and he would start to sing, tell a story, or play a tune on the mouthie (the harmonica), the Jew's harp, or the penny whistle. The entertainment was not at all one-sided. Guests would be pressed to make a contribution, so that the gathering exemplified an exhortation made famous by Duncan's cousin Betsy Whyte, in her autobiographical *The Yellow on the Broom*, to 'tell a story, sing a sang, show your bum, or oot ye gang!'

A Gaelic proverb asks: *Ciod iad na tri àitean a's fearr air son naidheachd? – Taigh-òsda, Muileann, agus Cèardach.*

What are the three best places for a story? – Hostelry, Mill and Smithy.

People of an older generation, who were brought up in rural communities which had a blacksmith, talk of what a great meeting place the smithy was – how the old men would gather there to discuss matters of the day, and the children dropped in on the way home from school to hear stories told round the fire. This November night in 2003, Duncan was convinced that, when the Lochcarron Smithy was a working forge, he had brought a horse there to be shod. Standing by the old anvil, with a peat fire sparking behind him, he told the story of The Boy and the Blacksmith, especially for the occasion. His audience gasped with horror and delight as the tale unfolded. Here it is, in Duncan's own words.

## ~ The Boy and the Blacksmith ~

A long time ago, away on the west coast, there lived an old black-smith and his name was John. And he had a tiny little blacksmith's shop, just like this, and he had a little cottage next to his black-smith's shop – and he had an old woman called Maggie.

Maggie was tall and thin, and she had a twist in her neck. Something had happened when she was young – her neck was twisted.

And John was a wee bit lazy. He was a wee bit overweight, and when you're overweight you get a wee bit lazy – that's true. And she was a nag, nag, nagging old woman. She said, 'Will you no go down to the smiddy and pump up the fire and do something, instead of sitting there watching me?'

To get out of her way he would go to the smiddy. He would pump up the fire and then he would sit back and relax, hoping no horses would come that day. But one morning, in through the door came a young man dressed in green, and he had a young woman across his shoulders. John was startled. He said, 'Can I help you, young man?'

He said, 'Blacksmith, I wonder if I could borrow your anvil?'

'There are no horses about. You can borrow the anvil if you like. What will you do with it?'

He said, 'Look, you just sit down there,' and he put his hand in his pocket and he took out five gold coins, and he said, 'There you are. That'll pay for what I'm gonnae do. But I'm only warning you. Never, never do what you see another person doing.'

John sat down in his chair. The young man went to the anvil with the young woman, and John looked. Her head was back to front! It was turned the opposite way round! And John said to him-self, 'What is he going to do?'

'Pay no attention to me. Just sit there. I'll pay you.' The young man said, 'Have you got a knife?'

John said, 'There are knives on the wall.'

'Are they sharp?'

John says, 'They're always sharp. They're for cutting horses' hooves! Help yourself.'

So he tries a few of the knives with his thumb, then he picks a long one. John says, 'What are you gonnae do?' And he puts the young woman's head on the anvil, and he cuts her head off. And her body falls on the floor. No blood, nothing. John's amazed.

The young man takes the young woman's head, and he puts it in the fire. And he pumps and he blows, and he pumps and he blows, and he pumps and he blows. And soon there's nothing left but white ash. Old John's sitting there mesmerised. And the young man takes a pair of tongs, and he takes out the head, and he puts it on the anvil. And he takes a hammer and pounds it. Soon there's a heap of dust on the anvil. John says, 'What is he going to do?' And then he spits on it, and he mixes it with his finger and makes a paste. And he walks over to the young woman, and there on her neck he puts the paste. And he sits back, and lo and behold a green glow begins to come off the paste, and took the form of a beautiful young woman. And her eyes opened and she smiled at the young man.

John was amazed. He's never seen anything like this before in his life. And the young man puts his arm round her, and he says, 'Thank you blacksmith. But remember, never do what you see another person doing.' And they were gone.

There was a knock at the door. 'Are you there, y'old bauchle?' It was Maggie, coming with his cup of tea, which she usually brought into the smiddy.

'Aye, I'm here,' says John.

'I've brought you your tea, you lazy old man. Is there nothing happening in the smiddy? What have you been doing? Sitting by the fire warming yourself?'

John says, 'Put the tea there on the bench.' And he took a sudden thought into his head. 'Mmm,' says he. He says, 'Maggie, come over here a minute.'

She says, 'What is it you want, y'old bauchle?'

He put his arms round her. She says, 'Take your hands off me!'

He grabs her. Over to the anvil with her. Picks up a knife – off with her head! And there's blood flowing all over the floor.

'I could do with something better,' he says, 'than her with the twisted neck. If he can do it, so can I.' And her body's lying on the floor, blood flowing everywhere. And he takes her head to the fire, and he pumps and he blows, and he pumps and he blows. Soon her old head's burnt to a cinder. And he collects it with a pair of

tongs, and he takes it back and he puts it on the anvil. And he tap, tap, taps, and soon it's a pile of dust. And he takes some spittle – he chews tobacco, it's tobacco spittle – and he mixes it with his finger. He puts it in the neck and he tries to put the head on, but it falls off on the floor. He tries again but it falls off again. What was he going to do? He had murdered his wife. There was only one answer. He has to bury her among the smiddy coal and clear out before anyone finds her. So he buries her body among the coals, puts the fire out, goes into the house, takes his wee bits of things he needs, locks the house up, and he's on his way. 'Never,' says he, 'will I show my face back there again, as long as I live.'

So he wandered far and wide, doing bits of jobs along the way. One year passed, then another year passed. He was far and miles away from where he'd left old Maggie, but nothing ever happened. But one day he seen a large town in the distance. He was broke. He had no tobacco, he had nothing. He saw an old man sitting on a seat, and he said, 'You wouldn't have a bit of tobacco to spare? I haven't had a chew for a long time.'

'I'll give you a bit of tobacco,' he said. 'Where are you bound for?'

'I'm going to the town,' says old John.

'Well,' he said, 'you'll really enjoy yourself there, 'cause it's the fair. What do you do for a living?'

'I'm a blacksmith.'

'Oh,' he says, 'there'll be plenty of work for a blacksmith. But it's a pity,' says he, 'it's a sad day, not the same as it is every fair.'

'Why's that?' says John.

'Well, you see, it's the King's daughter, the young Princess. Something strange has happened to her.'

'God bless me,' says John, 'what's happened to her?'

He says, 'Her head is back to front, and nobody can do anything for her. And the King's offered a large reward to anyone who can help his daughter.'

'Oh I see,' says old John, 'I see.' And he says to himself, maybe I could help. He makes his way through the town, makes his way to the palace, and he tells the guards he's come to help the King's daughter.

They say, 'What are you, a magician? People have been coming in their hundreds. Nobody can help her.'

'I want an appointment with the King himself. I have come to fix his daughter. I've come to make her right.'

'Very well,' they said. He got an appointment with the King.

The King said, 'You've come a long way. Where do you come from?'

John said, 'I come a way from the north, from the north of Scotland.'

'What do you do?' said the King.

'I'm a blacksmith.'

'It's not a blacksmith I'm looking for; it's a magician to help my daughter!'

'I can help your daughter,' said old John.

'Well,' said the King, 'if you don't help my daughter, and if anything happens to her, your head'll come from your shoulders so fast, you won't feel it coming off.'

John says, 'Don't worry. Do you have a blacksmith's shop nearby?'

'Of course we do. We need it for the horses.'

'Well,' says John, 'all you have to do is carry her down to the blacksmith's shop, and leave her with me. And I'll fix her for you, and she'll be as right as rain.'

'Oh, we'll carry her down,' says the King. 'But there'll be two guards outside the door. And if anything happens to my daughter, your head will come off so fast, you won't feel it coming off.'

'Don't worry,' says old John, 'I can fix her for you.'

So anyhow he got to the smiddy, off with his jacket, rolled up his sleeves, kindled up the fire, pumped until it was red hot. Two guards came down with a beautiful young lady. Eyes closed, head turned back to front. John goes to the smiddy wall, and he tries all the knives. And he comes to a real sharp one. Puts the Princess's head on the anvil and cuts it off. And he goes to the fire, and he puts the princess's head on the fire. And he pumps and he blows, and he pumps and he blows. 'It's got to work,' he says, 'it's got to work.'

And soon it's all burnt to a white ash. And he takes it out and he puts it on the anvil, and he goes tap, tap with his hammer. Soon there's a pile of dust on the anvil. But he doesn't mix it up this time with tobacco spittle; he mixes it with his finger with nice clean spittle, because it's the Princess. And soon there's a paste, and he takes some of the paste off the anvil and he puts it on her neck. And it falls on the floor. He picks it up off the floor and he puts it on her neck again. And it falls off again. Two guards are outside, waiting for the Princess. He begins to shiver with fear.

'What's going to happen to me?' he says. 'It's got to work, it's got to work.' He puts it on her neck, and it falls off again. And he gets a slap on the ear. And there, standing behind him, is the young man. He says, 'Didn't I tell you blacksmith, never to do what you see another person doing? Sit there, and don't move!' And he makes a little paste with the ash, and he takes the paste and he puts it on the Princess's neck. And then the glow comes, and the beautiful head appears again, on the top of the Princess, and she opens her eyes and she smiles. He puts his arm round her, as he done the very first time.

'Come on my dear, it's time to go. And you, remember! Never again! But this is for you.' And he puts seven gold coins in old John's palm. And he's gone.

And John sat there. And then he heard a knocking. 'Are you there, y'old bauchle? There's a man coming down the road with a horse. Here's your cup of tea.'

John opened his eyes, and there was old Maggie with her neck twisted. And he was so surprised he threw his arms round her.

She says, 'What are you at?'

'I want a kiss!' he says.

She says, 'You've never kissed me for years.'

'Well I'm going to kiss you now,' he says. 'I'm going to kiss you like I've never kissed you before in all my life.'

She says, 'Go on y'old bauchle. Here's your tea. There's a man coming down the road with a horse. Maybe we'll get some money to buy some food.'

He said, 'Money. Is it money you're worried about?' He put his hand in his pocket. Twelve gold coins.

She said, 'Have you been cheating on me y'old bauchle? Where did you get that from?'

He said, 'It's for you. And you'll get more when the man comes with the horse.'

And from that day until old John died, he never again said an angry word to his old woman. And he kissed her every night before he went to bed.

# ~ A Highland Origin Myth ~

The single-track road out of Lochcarron threads through the hills for a short while before it reaches the Bealach, a road which follows an old drovers' route. The Bealach is the steepest inclined road in Britain, ascending above Loch Kishorn in a series of hairpin bends to the top of Sgùrr a'Chaorachain and a view across to the Isle of Skye and the Cuillin mountains. Down below is the village of Applecross, where St Maelrubha, an Irishman from Derry, founded a monastery in the late seventh century.

The story doesn't begin or end here, but most of the action takes place in Applecross.

A long time ago – and I mean a very long time ago – Norway was full of giants. This was a situation left over from the time of the Norse gods, when the giants had their own territory, which was called Utgard. Though they weren't the brightest of beings, they managed quite well there, seldom coming unstuck unless one of them strayed into Asgard, the realm of the gods themselves, or unless one of the gods – Odin or Loki, and particularly Thor – made a foray into Utgard. Thor, who some might call a belligerent, red-bearded bully, was never happier than when he was laying into the giants with his famous hammer, Mjölnir.

Snorri Sturluson's *Edda* says that after Ragnarök, the battle to end all battles, both gods and giants perished, but this isn't entirely true. Many of the giants, male and female, had been far too slow on the uptake to get to Ragnarök in time for the final conflict, and they were left wandering aimlessly in a wasteland, waiting for the beginning of the world as we know it today. This is how, when civilisation did arrive, Norway came to be full of giants.

On the whole, giants and humans got on pretty well together. There was the occasional brawl – lady giants sometimes took a shine to gentleman humans – but disputes of that kind will arise in any close-knit community. Generally speaking, although a certain amount of mutual partying went on at the weekends, giants and humans tended to go home to their own beds and dream their respective dreams.

Just occasionally, though, a rogue giant would surface, and everything would be thrown off kilter. There was a giant called Thrim, a survivor from the bad old days, who hated humans. He lived high up in the mountains so, for a long time, he caused no trouble, but in time his hatred grew so intense that he began to make excursions down into the valley villages, rampaging around, biting off the heads of humans, sucking out their vital juices, and tossing away the skin and bone. As he advanced on an unsuspecting community or an isolated farmstead, Thrim would roar, 'I'm gonna find you! I'm gonna catch you! I'm gonna eat you!'

This behaviour was intolerable to both humans and giants, who had worked hard to live together in peace, so they convened a council and voted to expel Thrim from Norway.

Thrim wasn't greatly bothered by this decision. He was happy to follow his lust for human juice wherever it might lead him, so he headed out for the place we now call Scotland. The North Sea was much shallower then, and Thrim strode through waters which seldom rose above his knees, announcing as he went, 'I'm gonna find you! I'm gonna catch you! I'm gonna eat you!'

After a couple of days' wading, the giant reached Shetland. The islands were even more sparsely populated than they are today, and most of the inhabitants were trolls, or 'trows', more refugees from Ragnarök, who thought the universe had passed them by until Thrim came storming over the horizon. He didn't spend long in Shetland. In truth, the blood of the trows – green, viscous stuff – tasted so vile that even Thrim couldn't stomach it. He didn't bother to stop in Fair Isle – more trows – but there were enough humans on Orkney to detain him for a while. The few who escaped hopped into their boats and made for the mainland – for Caithness, as it's now called – leaving the islands as easy pickings for a Viking takeover a couple of millennia later. Once Orkney was devoid of humans, Thrim pursued the refugees across the Pentland Firth to Caithness. Splashing through the Swelkie whirlpool, he yelled at the distant mountains of Sutherland, 'I'm gonna find you! I'm gonna catch you! I'm gonna eat you!'

There's no precise record of the devastation that Thrim left in his wake on his progress across the Highlands. Occasionally archaeologists on a dig will come across an isolated skull which has no body nearby, and they will wonder about the strange rituals of our ancestors; and there are geological faults which can best be explained as resulting from the impact of giant footsteps. But all we know for sure is that eventually Thrim came to the west coast, to the Applecross peninsula in the region which is now called Wester Ross. The great mountain called Sgùrr a'Chaorachain – the big conical hill of the blaze or the torrent – comes between Applecross and the rest of the mainland. From the far side of Sgùrr a'Chaorachain, the people of Applecross heard the distant cry of the approaching giant, 'I'm gonna find you! I'm gonna catch you! I'm gonna eat you!' But they were prepared for his coming. For weeks, tales of the gargantuan bloodsucker had been brought in by refugees from other parts of the Highlands. The presence of these refugees had started to cause problems – overcrowding and food shortages – and some of the Applecross folk were all for putting them on makeshift rafts and sending them over the sea to Raasay and Skye; but the Community Council held an extraordinary meeting, and came up with a plan.

A broad, deep pit was dug in the place where the Applecross camp-site is today. Several dozen pine trees were felled and set in the bottom of the pit, then sharpened into massive stakes. For the next part of the plan, half a dozen of the cheekiest Applecross children were sent up Sgùrr a'Chaorachain. The goading, threatening voice of Thrim grew closer until, at last, a boulder-sized spiky head appeared above the highest peak, and the giant hove into view. As soon as they saw him, the cheeky children began to throw out taunts. 'Dim-wit lardybum' was the least of them.

The children, pursued by the raging, stumbling giant, skipped down the brae, across the heather and over the burns, knowing every inch of the land. At the bottom of the mountain they scattered. The giant, propelled by his own momentum, sped on downwards. The people of Applecross had stretched a tripwire across the path just before the stake pit. Thrim never even saw the wire (for giants are short-sighted). When his ankles hit it, he flew up into the air and revolved several times, before landing on the stakes, in the pit. With the giant impaled, the Applecross folk swarmed down, and set to work with whatever sharp implements they possessed. Pen-knives, hacksaws, hatchets, chainsaws were all used to dismember Thrim's body. After they had cut him into the tiniest pieces, they retired to the Applecross Inn to celebrate their victory, and in the early hours they straggled home to their beds. Some time in the night – nobody can remember exactly when – the people of Applecross were woken by a distant, muted voice. 'I'm gonna find you,' it whispered. 'I'm gonna catch you,' it murmured. 'I'm gonna eat you,' it mused.

Next morning, at dawn, they were out of their houses and down to the pit. There was no doubt that the tiny pieces of Thrim-flesh were still alive. They were jiggling around, and muttering angrily to themselves, 'I'm gonna find you… I'm gonna catch you… I'm gonna eat you…' The Applecross folk gathered as much kindling and dried seaweed as they could. They threw them into the pit, and tossed burning brands after them, and once there was a good blaze they fed it with chunks of peat. They watched all day until the fire slowly dwindled, and by evening there was nothing left at the bottom of the pit but a layer of fine ash.

The inhabitants of Applecross looked at each other in relief and began to speak for the first time in many hours. They agreed that they had done well to rid the world of the giant and felt it was time to celebrate (again) with a drink and a party. As they turned away from the pit a faint breeze came in from the sea, and lifted tiny specks of ash into the air. Each piece of ash began to speak, and thousands of little voices chorused, 'We're gonna find you… we're gonna catch you… we're gonna eat you.'

The ash cloud drifted towards the Applecross people. They began to run, pursued by a voracious horde which was, indeed, intent on eating them. These were the very first Highland midges. Although they began life in Applecross, they quickly spread up and down the west coast, out to the islands, and have even set up colonies in other parts of

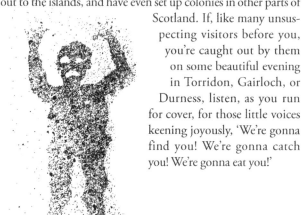

Scotland. If, like many unsuspecting visitors before you, you're caught out by them on some beautiful evening in Torridon, Gairloch, or Durness, listen, as you run for cover, for those little voices keening joyously, 'We're gonna find you! We're gonna catch you! We're gonna eat you!'

From Applecross the coast road heads directly north, then turns sharp east to Shieldaig and on to Torridon. A narrow road rises up out of Torridon, and through the mountains to Diabaig, whose name comes from the Old Norse, meaning a deep bay. Well into the twentieth century, the mail in these remote places was delivered on foot. Isabella Ross, who came to live in Diabaig when she was one year old, and who was the head teacher of Alligin Primary School from 1961, has a story about a postie that was passed down through her family. Here it is, in her own words.

In among the family was one called Murdo – Murdo Mackenzie. Now, for some unknown reason they gave him the nickname of 'Stabhais'. What it meant I don't know, but anyhow he was the postman; and even in my young days the postman left Diabaig at three o'clock in the afternoon and took the postbag over to Alligin. He met Buller, as they called him, who was coming with his push-bike to the Alligin post office. Mails were exchanged there, and the postman walked back to Diabaig. Now, he was due at work in Diabaig at nine o'clock, wasn't supposed to be any later than that, but on New Year's Night the postman could be as late as he liked. That was the one and only night in the year when the postman could take his time. So Murdo must have been taking his time on this particular New Year's Night.

Now I'm not going to say the Alligin people entertained him before he left – we don't know. But as you go to Diabaig, and as you come to the little loch on the top, and you go along past it, you'll see where the old road goes down by the side of the loch, and there is what they call Glac Stabhais, which means Stabhais's Hollow.

Now, whilst he was going along there, he saw this man, with the Mackenzie tartan kilt on, carrying his head under his arm. The postman was maybe a wee bit frightened, but he thought to himself, well… so he had this walking stick and he drew a circle round himself, and he said to this person, 'Now you're not coming inside that circle.' The ghost then spoke, and said that he was a chief of the Clan Mackenzie, and that long ago the MacLeods and the Mackenzies were disputing the land, but rather than the clansmen all fighting, the two chiefs decided that they would have a duel in this certain place. The chief of the Clan Mackenzie got there, and he was waiting for the chief of the Clan MacLeod to come, and he got fed up waiting and he fell asleep.

So the chief of the Clan MacLeod came along, and he thought to himself, 'Well I might lose this duel anyway. I'll just take pure advantage of him.' And he just took his sword and cut off his head.

The ghost said, 'My spirit couldn't rest until I appeared to someone of the Clan Mackenzie to tell them what happened.' He then disappeared. But before he disappeared he said, 'One year from now, a lump will grow on the back of your neck, and it's only then that you will tell your story.'

So the postman went home, didn't tell a soul. A year passed and one night this certain postman was up at the house of a man who was also called Murdo Mackenzie, getting his hair cut; and as Murdo the barber was cutting the other man's hair he said to him, 'What lump have you got on the back of your neck?'

So Murdo the postman said, 'Oh, is there a lump on the back of my neck?'

'Oh goodness yes, can you not feel it?'

'Oh well,' he said, 'now I can tell my story.'

So then he told his story. Then everybody, of course, began to be frightened of the ghost that he'd seen a year ago.

So time went on, and people began to make fun of him, and his brother became postman in his place. He gave up the job and he began working at the salmon fishing at Craig along with my grandfather. They used to stay in a bothy there during the week, and they just came home for the weekends. But sometimes during the week, when the days were long as they are just now, they maybe came to cut peats, or do something about the croft. And one evening they had been in Diabaig, and they walked back to Craig, and they were both sitting in the bothy. And as they were sitting there, the two of them, my grandfather said to him, 'Now Murdo,' he said, 'you and I have been friends for a very long time. Did you really see something that night coming from Alligin, and if you did, how did you dare to go back the following night?'

Murdo looked at my grandfather, and he said, 'If you knew the end of the story, you wouldn't be a bit surprised as to why I went back the following night. Neither you nor anybody else will ever know the end of the story.'

Well, Murdo Mackenzie, he was still quite a young man and, because people were making fun of him, he emigrated to New Zealand. He got work there on a sheep farm, and one day when he was out on a horse rounding up the sheep, he fell off it and he was killed. So that was the end of the postie.

The road from Torridon leads to Kinlochewe, where it meets the A832 which runs north-west along the side of Loch Maree, through Gairloch and on to Poolewe, the site of Inverewe Gardens, the exotic creation of Sir Osgood Mackenzie. To the west of Poolewe is the Inverasdale peninsula. Among the oak woods around Loch an Draing, in the far north of the peninsula, lived a creature who was known as the Gille Dubh, the Black Lad. Few people ever saw him, but those who had said that he was tall and broad and clothed himself in leaves, and that sometimes he wore a wreath of foliage around his head. In truth he kept as far away as he could from humans, but that didn't stop him being turned into a kind of bogeyman, whose name would be used by mothers to frighten their children into obedience. 'If you don't go to sleep right now, the Gille Dubh will come for you,' they would say.

A young family lived in a cottage in the oak woods. The father was an employee of the Laird Mackenzie, who owned all the lands round Poolewe, and he and his wife had one child, a daughter called Jessie. She was a sturdy character and an early walker. One summer's day, when her mother's back was turned, she wandered off into the woods. In those days there were still wolves in the Highlands, but Jessie had no idea that there might be danger. She loved the song of the birds, and the creatures which rustled unseen among the undergrowth, and she carried on toddling further and further away from home until it began to grow dark.

The nature of the birdsong changed, as owls called to each other and hunted among the treetops, and the rustlings in the under-growth became a sinister threat. Jessie, like one of the Babes in the Wood, sat with her back to the trunk of an oak and began to cry. She cried for a long time, while a big, round yellow moon rose up in the sky. When her exhausted weeping had dwindled to occasional sobs she heard the crunch of giant footsteps coming closer. A massive shadow rose up before her and blocked out the moon. Jessie was scooped up by a great hand and carried off into the woods to a shelter of branches, where she spent the night cradled safely in huge, leaf-clad arms. At dawn the Gille Dubh took her back to the edge of the clearing where her parents had their cottage, and gently set her down.

Time passed. The oak woods burgeoned, lost their leaves and burgeoned again, many times. Jessie's parents had died and she herself was a young married woman, soon to be a mother for the first time, and living in the cottage where she had been brought up. It was late on a spring afternoon. Jessie was taking in the washing when she heard the sound of voices coming up the track that led past the cottage. Her husband was on the hill, and wouldn't be back until the next day, and it worried her that strangers might be abroad in the woods when she was alone.

A party of men was on the track, and they had guns over their shoulders. When they were closer Jessie saw that it was Mackenzie the Laird, and his pals. The previous evening they had been talking about hunting, and the matter of the Gille Dubh was raised. Mackenzie had decided that the Black Lad's head would look good among the other trophies on his wall, so that morning he and his companions had set off in high spirits to hunt the creature down. However, they spent far too long at lunch in the inn, and were the worse for it. The hunt had scarcely begun, night was coming on and they were looking for a place to shelter.

Jessie took the washing inside and waited. The cottage door was swung back, and the rough crew marched in. They sat without being invited to sit, and a couple of them put their feet up on the table. Then they demanded food and drink. Jessie brought them bread and cheese, and took a bottle full of a pale amber liquid from the cupboard. The Laird and his friends ate and talked loudly at the same time, spluttering their food across the board. They seemed hardly aware that Jessie was present, but she understood well what they were planning to do. It wasn't too long before their heads were nodding on their chests, for they had no idea that the whisky they had drunk was from a still high up on the hillside, and more than usually potent.

When she was sure they were all asleep, Jessie left the cottage and went to the edge of the woods. It was a quiet, cool evening, with a powdering of stars over the sky and a sliver of old moon just above the trees. Jessie whispered into the darkness, 'Gille Dubh, Gille

Dubh.' She waited. There was a rustle of branches, twigs cracked, and the Gille Dubh stood up before her. Jessie took his hand and led him to the steading. When they were inside she made a sign that he should lie down in a corner, and when he was curled up she covered him over with straw. Then she went quietly into the house, and to bed.

Next morning the hunters set off into the woods. They scarcely said a word, and certainly didn't thank Jessie for her hospitality, for their heads were still thick with the previous night's indulgence. Jessie waited all day and, late in the afternoon, she heard disgruntled voices coming from among the trees. The Laird and his cronies were returning from their Gille Dubh hunt, guns still over their shoulders and not a single shot fired.

When they were out of sight and out of hearing, Jessie went into the steading and lifted the straw she had carefully arranged the night before. The Gille Dubh rose. Jessie took his hand and led him to the edge of the forest. Without looking back he shambled away into the trees, and that was the last time anyone saw him.

## ~ The Stalker ~

Hector Urquhart, who was one of the correspondents of the great Victorian gatherer of folk tales, John Francis Campbell, wrote in 1860 about his boyhood experiences of storytelling in Poolewe, where he was brought up:

> …when I was a boy, it was the custom for the young people to assemble together on the long winter nights to hear the old people recite the tales or *sgeulachd*, which they learned from their fathers before them. In these days tailors and shoemakers went from house to house, making our clothes and shoes. When one of them came to the village we were greatly delighted, whilst getting new kilts at the same time. I knew an old tailor who used to tell a new tale every night during his stay in the village; and another, an old shoemaker, who, with his large stock of stories about ghosts and fairies, used to frighten us so much that we scarcely dared pass the neighbouring churchyard on our way home. It was also the custom when an *aoidh*, or stranger, celebrated for his store of tales, came on a visit to the village, for us, young and old, to make a rush to the house where he spent the night, and choose our seats, some on beds, some on forms, and others on three-legged stools etc., and listen in silence to the new tales; just as I have myself seen since, when a far-famed actor came to perform in the Glasgow theatre. The goodman of the house usually opened with the tale of the Famhair Mòr (great giant) or some other favourite tale, and then the stranger carried on after that. It was a common saying, 'The first tale by the goodman, and tales to daylight by the *aoidh*,' or guest.

The following is one of the kinds of story that would have been told during these gatherings. Such stories are sometimes called 'wonder tales' and are widely dispersed throughout many countries. This is based on a version taken down by Hector Urquhart himself in 1859, from the telling of John Campbell, a sawyer. Campbell lived in Strath Gairloch, which is not far from Poolewe.

There was a widow's son, who was always up on the hill stalking. One afternoon he was leaning up against a grassy mound, sheltering from the wind and enjoying the warmth of the sun, when he saw, way up the track, a horse and rider coming towards him. It was a handsome young man, riding a blue filly. The young man dismounted and began a conversation with the Stalker. One thing led to another, and a game of cards was proposed. As the afternoon wore on, the Stalker was doing pretty well. The stakes got higher, the Stalker and the young man ended up playing for the blue filly, and the Stalker won her. Who knows what happened to the handsome young man, but the Stalker rode the filly home and, as he was tethering her outside his house, she turned into the most beautiful woman he had ever seen. That night, in his bed, they became one.

Next morning the Stalker kissed his new wife goodbye and went up on the hill. At the end of the day when he came over the ridge and looked down on his house, he saw that the thatch had been ripped away and the furniture inside scattered about. When he got down there, there was no sign of his wife. A neighbour came out. She had seen everything. 'A giant took her,' she said.

At dawn the Stalker set off to find his wife. He travelled all day. He travelled down the deepest, darkest glens, and across rushing torrents. He travelled over the highest mountain peaks, through rain and hail and sleet and snow. As evening approached he came to a little hut on a hillside. The hut was thatched entirely with birds' feathers, feathers of hoodies on the outside and wrens on the inside. He went in. The floor was even and smooth. There were two big fires burning, and a table and a chair, but no sign of any animal or any human being. Out of the corner of his eye he saw something flying in through the door. It was a falcon holding a duck, which it dropped on the table. Then, as the Stalker watched, the falcon turned into a boy with a sharp nose and piercing blue eyes.

'Your wife was here last night with a big giant,' said the boy. 'Things weren't looking so good for her.'

'That's why I'm here,' said the Stalker. 'I'm on their trail, and woe to that giant when I catch up with them.'

'You'll catch up with them, sure enough. But before you leave you must eat and rest.'

They roasted the duck and shared it between them. Then the Stalker lay down in front of the fires. 'What will happen,' he said, 'if anything wicked comes by in the night?'

'Don't worry,' said the boy, 'I'll be watching over you.'

When the Stalker woke at first light there was more food cooked and waiting on the table – this time a couple of blackcocks. After they had eaten, the boy said to the Stalker, 'You should get on your way now. Good luck with your search, and if you ever need my help, just call on the Blue-eyed Falcon of Glen Feist.'

On the second day the glens were deeper and darker, and the mountain passes higher and steeper. As night came down the Stalker arrived at a little hut. This hut was thatched with the feathers of ravens on the outside and the feathers of finches on the inside. He entered. There were two fires burning, and a table and chair, but he was the only living creature there. Out of the corner of his eye he saw something bounding in through the door. It was an otter, and in its mouth was a fat salmon. The otter stood on its back legs and dropped the salmon onto the table; then, as the Stalker watched, the otter turned into a young man with a sleek thatch of brown hair.

'I saw your wife here last night with a big giant,' said the young man. 'She wasn't looking so happy.'

'That's why I'm here,' said the Stalker. 'I'm on their trail, and when I catch up with them that giant will be sorry.'

'You're getting closer, but you should eat and sleep before you set off again.'

So they cooked and ate the salmon, then the Stalker slept while the young man watched over him. In the morning there were two roasted trout on the table for breakfast. When the trout were down to the bones, the young man said, 'You should be away now. Good luck with your search, and if you ever need my help, call on Brown Otter of Sail Stream.'

On the third day the glens were so deep the Stalker could smell the brimstone, and the mountains so high he could hear the music of harps. It was in the dead of night that he saw a light far off. When he came to it, there was a hut, thatched on the outside with eagles' feathers and on the inside with the feathers of larks. He went in and sat at the table, before the two fires, and waited. A big grey hound leapt in through the door with a hare in its mouth. It tossed the hare high in the air, and the hare landed on the table. Then, as the Stalker watched, the hound turned into a wiry, grey-haired man, who said, 'Your wife was here last night along with a big giant. She certainly didn't seem pleased to be in his company.'

'That's why I'm here,' said the Stalker. 'It won't be long before I catch up with that giant, and when I find him, he'll rue the day.'

'You're right,' said the grey-haired man, 'it won't be long now; but you should eat and sleep before you set off.'

They roasted the hare and shared its meat; then the Stalker lay down in front of the fires and went to sleep, while the grey-haired man watched over him.

As the Stalker was getting ready to leave, the wiry, grey-haired man said, 'You don't have far to go now. If you ever need my help, just call on Grey Dog of the Mountain. Remember now.'

The Stalker set off on the fourth day of his journey. The glens were so deep he could feel the heat of the fires of hell, and the mountains were so high he could hear the beating of the angels' wings. By late afternoon, when the sun was casting long shadows, he came to a ravine, and at the bottom of the ravine was a long white house. The Stalker took out his spyglass and scanned the windows of the house, and through one of them he saw his wife with a comb in her hand. Alternately she combed her hair and wept.

There was a steep, narrow path down to the bottom of the ravine. The Stalker descended. Pebbles rattled about his feet. As he crossed the burn that ran in front of the white house, a window opened and his wife leant out. 'What are you doing here? If the giant sees you, he'll kill you.'

'What did you expect me to do? I love you too much to let a giant steal you away from me.'

He climbed in through the window, and they kissed and talked for a while. Then they heard the thunderous footsteps of the giant as he entered the house. He had been out in the woods and was returning home for his tea.

'Come with me,' said the Stalker's wife, and she hid him under the bed.

'What's that smell?' said the giant when he came into the room. 'Smells like human.'

'A magpie dropped a bone down the chimney into the fire. I threw it out, but the stink still lingers.'

After supper, the Stalker's wife cuddled up to the giant. 'There's something I wish you would tell me.'

'What's that?'

'I know your heart isn't in your body. I know you keep it hidden. I wish you'd tell me where that secret hiding place is.'

The giant grunted. 'Well, if you must know, my heart is in the grey cairn at the back of the house.'

Next morning, as soon as the giant was off to the woods, the Stalker and his wife went out to the back of the house and took the grey cairn apart stone by stone – but there was no sign of any heart. When they had put the stones back in place, the Stalker's wife picked wild flowers and scattered them over the cairn. They weren't long in the house when they heard the giant returning from the woods, so the Stalker hid under the bed.

The giant entered the room. 'What's that smell? Why are there flowers on the grey cairn?'

'A magpie dropped another bone down the chimney. And the flowers are on the cairn because I know you keep your heart there, and I wanted to show how much I love you.'

'Hummph,' said the giant, 'lots of bones coming down this chimney.'

After they'd eaten, the Stalker's wife cuddled up to the giant. 'Is there something bothering you? Is there something you want to tell me?'

'Not really. Well, I did tell you a bit of a fib. Last night, when we were cuddling, I told you I kept my heart in the grey cairn, and it wasn't really true. Well, it wasn't true at all.'

'Never mind. I expect you were testing me.'

'I was testing you, but I feel bad that I didn't tell you the truth.'

'You can tell me now.'

'My heart is in that old tree stump, out in the garden.'

Next morning, as soon as the giant had set off for the wood, the Stalker and his wife went out into the garden to find the tree stump. They took the giant's axe with them. The stump was massive, but it only took the Stalker three blows to split it open. A hare jumped out, and ran off into the woods.

'Grey Dog of the Mountain!' called the Stalker, and the grey dog shot out of the undergrowth, coursing through the trees. It caught the hare by the scruff, and with a single shake snapped its neck, then brought it to the Stalker and laid it down at his feet. The Stalker took his hunting knife and slit open the hare's belly, and a fat salmon slipped out, wriggled over the grass into the burn, and began to swim upstream.

'Brown Otter of Sail Stream!' called the Stalker and a square head with two beady black eyes surfaced in the water. The otter overtook the salmon, caught it gently between its jaws and brought it to the Stalker. He cut open the fish, and a duck flew out of its belly and away up into the sky.

'Blue-eyed Falcon of Glen Feist!' The falcon dropped out of a cloudless sky and hit the duck like a thunderbolt. Out of the duck came one white egg which tumbled down and down until the Stalker's wife caught it. She had it in her grasp – the giant's heart.

Way off in the forest, thunder rolled. It was the giant, storming through the trees. As he came towards the Stalker's wife she held up the egg between a finger and thumb, so he could see it clearly. His eyes grew as wide as plates, and he cried out, 'Don't break my heart!'

The Stalker's wife, who had once been a blue filly, took the egg in her palm and squeezed hard. The egg broke, the yolk dribbled down her arm, and the giant dropped like a felled pine.

'There,' she said.

So the Stalker and his wife took one of the giant's horses and set off on their four-day journey. They travelled down the deepest, darkest glens, and over the highest mountain peaks, until at last they arrived back home. After they settled in, they threw a party for all the neighbours, and the last time I passed by there, it was still going on.

## Big Hughie Kilpatrick

The A832 winds north from Poolewe, round Loch Ewe and Gruinard Bay, then along the south side of Little Loch Broom. Opposite the Scoraig peninsula you come to a place called Camusnagaul – the bay of the Lowlander, or perhaps of the Englishman. Close to Camusnagaul there once lived a legendary character, who is still spoken of today. He was called Uisdean Mòr Mac 'Ille Phàdruig – Big Hughie Kilpatrick. As his name suggests, Big Hughie was a man of monumental stature, and nothing could scare him, whether it came from the world of men or from the realm of the spirits. In some accounts of his life, he is said to have been a professional bogle-hunter. Big Hughie is mentioned in John Francis Campbell's *Popular Tales of the West Highlands*, and Alec Williamson, the great Traveller storyteller, also has tales about him.

Uisdean Mòr often travelled to Inverness on business (even today there are a lot of bogles in Inverness). Returning home from one of these journeys on a black, stormy evening, he was on the Dirriemore, a bleak stretch of country between Loch Droma and the Corrieshalloch Gorge, when he saw something lying across the track ahead of him. As he got closer he realised it was a woman, and that she was pregnant and about to give birth. What she was doing on the Dirrie so late on such a night, Big Hughie asked himself, but his next thought was that he must save her from perishing in such an unlikely place.

At that time there were wild horses on the Dirriemore. Big Hughie caught and killed one of them, then slit open its belly and took out its innards. He gathered heather and used it to line the horse's insides, then lifted the woman into the warm nest he had made for her. He tied the forelegs and the back legs of the horse together, lifted the animal onto his shoulders, and made for the nearest habitation. When he entered the cottage the horse's hooves were the first thing to appear out of the darkness, and, according to Alec Williamson, the people thought it was the Devil himself entering.

When he had made sure the woman was going to be well looked after, Big Hughie went on his way, back home to Camusnagaul. Some months later he was looking out of the window across Little Loch Broom, when he saw a boat approaching the shore. A woman carrying a baby climbed out of the boat and came up to his door. It was the woman he had saved on the Dirriemore and she had come to thank him. She had given birth to a boy. Every so often the two would come over the water to visit Big Hughie. When the boy got bigger, he used to say, 'Today I came to see you in a boat, but once I was in the belly of my mother, in the belly of a horse.'

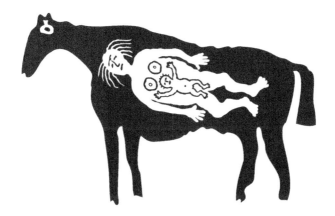

That's Alec Williamson's version of the story. I have heard another ending; that as he grew older, Big Hughie became down on his luck and took to the road. He found himself wandering the streets of Edinburgh, when a voice called to him in Gaelic. He looked up, and it was the woman from the Dirriemore, now wealthy and living in the city. She took him in and gave him shelter in return for his kindness all those years before.

Alec has two more tales of Big Hughie Kilpatrick. In the first, Big Hughie was on his way from Camusnagaul to Inverness. He came to Garve, where there is a ford in the river. In Big Hughie's time this was often spoken of as a dangerous place. The keeper of the crossing was a little tailor and, if you refused to pay him, when you were halfway across the river, a gigantic buck goat would appear and put an end to you.

On this day, Big Hughie got to the crossing and the tailor slipped out from behind a rock demanding his toll, but Uisdean Mòr was having none of it. The tailor reminded him that, if he didn't pay, he would have the buck goat to contend with.

'Never mind,' said Big Hughie. 'I have my sword.'

'What if the sword sticks in the scabbard?'

'Well then, I have my pistol.'

'And what if the pistol jams?'

'Then I have my Grand Aunt.'

'Your Grand Aunt?'

'Aye, my Grand Aunt, she'll come to my rescue.'

Confounded, the tailor slipped away, and Big Hughie started to cross the river. Halfway over, a the buck goat came striding towards him, taller than a man and walking on its hind legs. Big Hughie tried to draw his sword but it stuck in the scabbard. He pulled the pistol from his belt, aimed, and squeezed the trigger, but it refused to fire. So he reached down, slipped the *sgian dubh* – the black-handled knife – from its sheath in the top of his hose, and plunged it into the goat's chest. The goat shrieked and staggered back onto the bank and off into the trees, and Big Hughie continued on his way to Inverness.

A couple of weeks later, returning through Garve, Big Hughie asked after the tailor. The people were very sad. The tailor's sick, they said. We think he's dying, and who will guard the ford when he's gone?

Big Hughie went to the tailor's house and entered without knocking. The tailor was lying in bed, deathly pale. Hughie pulled back the sheets. The tailor had a chest wound in exactly the place where Hughie had stabbed the goat.

'I knew it, you monster. It's you that's been turning yourself into the buck goat all these years, terrifying people. Now you're dying and that's all you deserve.'

The tailor was a wizard. When he had asked Big Hughie what weapons he would use against the buck goat, Hughie had named both the sword and the pistol, which had allowed the tailor to put a spell on them; but Big Hughie knew what the tailor was up to, and had kept the identity of the *sgian dubh* secret, calling it his Grand Aunt. So the tailor had been powerless against the *sgian dubh*, and that's what had finished him off. Under the bed was a chest full of the money the tailor had cheated out of the people. Big Hughie distributed it among them before he went on his way, back to Camusnagaul.

The last story is more about the big man's son, than it is about Hughie himself. This son was a feeble creature, who was scared of the dark. His father was determined that he would toughen him up.

Not far from Camusnagaul was a cave which was the haunt of the *Fuath*, who were the aboriginal inhabitants of the Highlands. They were big, hairy creatures, close relatives of Bigfoot in North America and the Abominable Snowman of the Himalayas, and they had been in the region long before humans. Big Hughie took his

son, bound hand and foot, to the cave, and left him there for the night. For a long time the boy lay there, listening to the owls calling across the glen, and the hissing of shooting stars. The inside of the cave was bright with the light of a barely waning moon.

Some time after midnight a shadow passed in front of the moon and a large, hairy creature came into the cave, followed by two more of the same kind. It was the *Fuath* returning home from their rambles. They put their shaggy heads together, and began to speak in Gaelic, in deep, melancholy voices.

'We are the last of our kind,' said the leader. 'The wolf, the beaver, the bear and the wild pig have all gone before us, and we will be the next to go.'

'Who's that in the corner?' said another.

'That's the son of Uisdean Mòr Mac 'Ille Phàdruig.'

'He looks in a sorry state.'

'He is that, but I'll tell you something. He will never die until he sets foot on Italian soil.'

And that was that. Some time later the *Fuath* quit the cave and, in the morning, Big Hughie came to take his son back home. The harsh treatment seemed to have worked. The boy was no longer afraid of the dark, and grew up to be a solid, upstanding character, a great worthy. He married and had children, and they had children in their turn. In time his wife passed away, but he continued to live into a terrible old age. He became hard of hearing and could scarcely see, and he spent his days sitting on a chair in the porch of the family home.

One day some of his great grandchildren came running up to the house. They tugged him by the sleeve and told him to come and see what they had found on the loch shore. He took his stick and tottered down, supported by the children, and there was a piece of turf just the length of his body. It was ballast that had been jettisoned by a ship which was heading for Ullapool, and that ship had come from Italy. He lay down on the turf and, with one sigh, he gave up the spirit.

# TRAVELS
# AND TRAVAILS

The A835 runs north-west from the Tore roundabout on the A9. It passes through Garve, where Big Hughie Kilpatrick encountered the buck goat, and along the Dirriemore where, on a stormy night, he came upon the woman who was about to give birth. The road passes along the side of Loch Broom and through the port of Ullapool, where Ulli the Viking once had his farmstead, then heads north to join the A837 at Ledmore Junction.

This is one of the routes taken by the family of Alec Williamson, in the days when they travelled the roads of Ross-shire, Sutherland, Skye and Caithness. Alec, whose contribution to this book has been invaluable, is one of the last of the old-style Highland Travellers, known historically as 'tinkers' or 'tinklers', because of their metal-working skills. As well as stories, his repertoire includes songs, place name lore, riddles, jokes, tongue twisters, anecdotes and verse.

Ailig Iain MacUilleim – Alec John Williamson – was born in Rheguile, a little hilltop community above Edderton in Ross-shire, in '1932, the last day of December, Hogmanay night. My granny was the midwife, gave me a skelp on the bum, and I took to the bottle right away!' His father and his mother were both Gaelic speakers, and when he first went to school, the young Alec knew only three words in English, 'Yes and No and Me, but I didn't know when to use them.' Now he is the last of his branch of the Williamsons to speak Gaelic.

In Alec's youth, the Highland Travellers would spend the winter months in a settled place and take to the road in the spring. They travelled by horse and cart, lived in tents and made their living as tinsmiths – Alec's father was one – horse dealing, hawking, pearl fishing and working for the farmers. The children had official dispensation to take time off from school to travel, during the summer. 'Once you would hear the birds singing, something stirred in your blood; you'd want to get away again, to travel the roads. You see, you could take the Traveller out of the road, but you couldn't take the road oot o' the Traveller.'

Alec's mother passed away on the Isle of Skye, when he was four, and after that his father raised the children single-handed. The family continued travelling until the 1950s, 'but there wasn't a right living to be done on it then. The plastic came in. This did away with tin. Things was getting mechanised. This did away with the horses.' So an old, semi-nomadic way of life came to an end.

It was during the winter, round the hearth at Garden Cottage – the house his father had built in Rheguile – that Alec heard most of the stories he tells today. 'When we would be away in the summer time, there wasna' that many stories going because people were busy. But in the winter nights, when we would be at our own settled place, that's when you would hear them.'

Alec will often say that he was 'either cursed, or blessed, with a long memory. I can remember back to three year old, you see, and I can remember when my mother was in the house, and some of her sayings, I can remember it.' His favourite storyteller was his father, from whom he inherited a talent for telling the same stories equally vividly in both Gaelic and English. 'When I'm telling a story, it's just the same as reading a story. You're there! That's the way it is with me. I've got to be there, I imagine myself there.'

The next couple of stories are from Alec Williamson, told in his own words. The first ranges across the Atlantic and back, though it begins not far north of Ullapool in Glutan Glen, a bleak gorge of a place. The Tiger-Striped Dog starts in Polbain, opposite the Summer Isles on the Achiltibuie peninsula, but most of the action is played out further inland, on a plain next to the A835, just south of the Achiltibuie turn off. In this second story, Loch Lurgainn is 'the loch of the shins', so-called because Finn MacCool threw what remained of his mother's legs in the water, when the rest of her body had been destroyed during a battle with giants from Garve.

Talking aboot Glutan, this is a wee glen as you leave Strathcanaird. There was a man there – there's only one house that's in Glutan – and he was named Roddy, but I don't know his second name. I think he must have been Mackenzie or MacLeod, must have been, but they called him 'Roddy Glutan'. The man wasn't a glutton, but that was the name of the place, you know.

And he left his wife and his family. I don't know how many family he had, but there was no television in them days, so he might have had a few. Anyway, he went to America. He landed on the Atlantic Seaboard.

His wife was waiting for money to come back. No money was coming, no money at all, and no word was coming. So now the oldest of the boys he grew up a bit, and he said, 'Look Mum,' he said, 'I'm going to America.'

'What?' she said. 'You know what your dad did.'

'Aye,' he said, 'but I'll no do the same as that. I will write you back. I'm going to America.' So he did.

Now he travelled the northern states, Massachusetts and Illinois, and he was trying to find out where his father was. But he couldn't find out where he was.

Anyway he got work, he got up a bit of money and now he went over to Boston, got back oot o' there, and he took him to Chicago. And he was passing this saloon. He was hearing a song going, and when he listened to the song it was a Gaelic song, and he had heard it before. So he went in, and this man was standing at the counter saying, 'Anybody here that can sing that song?'

'I can sing that song. Sing it maybe better than you.'

'Who are you?' said the man at the counter.

'Don't you know me?'

'No,' he said.

He said, 'I come from Glutan Glen. That's not very far from Ullapool. I'm your son,' he said, 'and you never wrote my mother, you never sent anything home to the children.'

'No,' he said, 'I didn't.'

'And did you think I wouldn't know that song? I know it,' he said, 'and that's how I found you. Now tomorrow,' he said, 'you're coming down with me, and I'm going to put you on board a ship.'

He said, 'You don't need. I have no money to take me home.'

'I have money,' said his son, 'and I'm going to send you home.'

And he got him to the ship, and he sent him home – he got him on it, and he sent him home to Glutan, near Ardmair. And you know this, I don't think he ever went oot o' the hoose again.

And that's the story of Roddy Glutan.

# ⁓ The Tiger-Striped Dog ⁓

There's a place in Achiltibuie called Polbain. Many a time I called there, many a time I hawked it. And there was a man there. Aonghas Donn they called him in Gaelic, and that is the equivalent of Brown-haired Angus. And I came to his door one time, and I said, 'I'm looking for Aonghas Donn.'

And the daughter came out, and she said, 'Aonghas Donn. Oh yes.'

Then he shouted from inside, 'Ah well boy, I was Aonghas Donn at one time, but now I'm Grey-haired Angus. Come in!'

Anyway, his grandfather in Polbain was telling my grandfather one time. He said, 'In spring time, we had the horses oot on what we call the Common. And they were on the hills there, and they would travel for miles, you know. 'We were needing the horse,' he said, 'so I went to get it.'

'Now,' he said, 'I came past Bad a'Ghaill, I came past Loch Lurgainn, and away along there's a plain there, and it comes from Drumrunie, Strathcanaird, right down. And I didn't take my jacket. It was hot weather, and I had a shirt on, with short sleeves on it, and I saw this coming across the plain. I first thought it was a stray dog, but as it was coming nearer I could tell that he never had anything to do with humans.'

'So, I came nearer and he came towards me, and he caught me by the arm. I had nothing to save myself. I hadn't got a knife, I hadn't got a gun, I had nothing. He went at the arm and he started chewing it. But I put my hand in my pocket and there was this little toy of a thing, a wee penknife. And I took it out, and I got it unclasped with my teeth. I stuck it there, in his neck, as hard as it would go,' he said.

'So now, the dirtiest sight that I ever saw was the dog's blood and my blood mixed, but I kept screwing the knife, because there wasn't much of a blade on it. The dog dropped,' he said, 'and bled to death. So I pulled off the shirt I had on, and I made a sling of it for my arm, and I came back home. I couldn't take the horse, I was in that much pain, so I came back to Achiltibuie, and I went to Polbain, to my house. And a doctor was called for, and he said I'd got most of the poison out.'

'But the dog,' he said, 'I can never get over. It was his colour. He was tiger-striped. I never saw a dog tiger-striped in my life. But I done away with him.'

And he said to my grandfather, 'Do you know this, there's hills up there – go up to Cul Beag, Cul Mòr, even over Quinag – and you'd be very surprised at what you would see or meet in that hills yet.'

So that is the end of that story. And I didn't know the man it happened to, but I did know his grandson.

Continuing north from the plain where Aonghas Donn's grand-father encountered the Tiger-Striped Dog – into the county of Sutherland and the shores of Loch Assynt – Ardvreck Castle is situated on a spit of land at the east end of the loch, close to the famous Bone Caves of Inchnadamph. The name comes from the Gaelic, An Àird Bhreac, which means the speckled promontory. The castle is an impressive Gothic ruin now, but it was once a compact three-storey dwelling with cellars and an attic, and possibly a courtyard and a walled garden as well.

The castle was built by the MacLeods, a little over 400 years ago. Its construction was the outcome of a deal with the Devil, says one legend. In return for having it built, MacLeod pledged the hand of his daughter to the Dark One Himself. After the marriage, when she found out the true identity of her husband, the girl drowned herself in the loch, and her ghost is still seen on the shore from time to time.

Ardvreck Castle is best known as the place where James Graham, the Marquis of Montrose, was captured in 1650 and handed over to the Covenanters. Betrayed by clans he thought were allies, Graham – together with his Royalist army of continental mercenaries and militarily inexperienced Orcadians – had been routed at Carbisdale in the east. Wounded, he made his way across country to Ardvreck disguised as a shepherd. Some versions of the story say he was betrayed again, this time by Neil MacLeod, who offered him hospitality and then turned him in; but the MacLeods have denied this as malicious propaganda. Whatever the truth behind his apprehension, Montrose was taken to Edinburgh, where he was hanged at the town cross. Afterwards, parts of his dismembered body were sent to be displayed in Glasgow, Perth, Stirling and Aberdeen.

One night in 1672, when the occupants were away, Mackenzies from Applecross came ashore, set fire to Ardvreck Castle and took possession of Assynt. This, history says, is how the castle came to be in its present ruinous state.

But there's another, more legendary, explanation for the dilapidation. It tells of the Lady of Ardvreck, the old woman who was the castle's owner, whose particular talent was for setting folk against each other. She had managed to stir up discord among most of her neighbours, but one young man, who had a light-hearted and forgiving nature, had been impervious to her cantrips. Finally, though, he succumbed. His wife had recently given birth – the baby was so new it was still unbaptised – and the old woman had been putting it about that he was not the father. She didn't say this directly. Instead she would remark to acquaintances of the young man upon the child's striking resemblance to a gentleman who lived over the mountains in Kylesku, who was notorious as a rambling philanderer. The acquaintances would pass on these insinuations. Of course, they would express horror that such vile lies were being spread around – someone should do something to silence the old witch – but the plan worked well enough. The worm of suspicion ate into the young man's heart, and eventually he openly accused his wife of cuckolding him.

The tears, the denials, the utter estrangement between the couple that resulted from the accusation, led the young woman to call on her two brothers for support. They lived a good distance away, but hurried to be with their embattled sister. When they arrived at her home they immediately tried to persuade the young husband of his wife's innocence, but he would have none of it.

The younger brother had spent time in Italy. In the Black School of Padua his tutor had been the Old Lad Himself, so he felt more than equipped to cope with the wiles of the Lady of Ardvreck. Early on a bright spring morning, the two brothers and the young husband walked up to the castle entrance. The loch was smooth as a looking glass, and reflected a cloudless sky. They knocked, and a servant girl let them in. She took them to the hall, a room whose walls, floor and ceiling were clad entirely in stone. The Lady of Ardvreck rose to greet them. 'You've come on a mission,' she said.

'Indeed we have,' said the younger brother. 'These tales about our sister's husband and the parentage of his child – people say they come from you. Surely this can't be the case.'

'The truth must be told. What kind of a world would we live in if the truth was not available to all?'

'Shall we call upon an arbitrator whom we both know well?'

'Summon him,' said the Lady of Ardvreck.

The younger brother took his staff and drew an invisible circle on the stone flags. He muttered words that no one in the room understood; apart, perhaps, from the old woman. Outside, the sky grew dark. The surface of the loch began to heave. A huge wave rose up and smacked against the side of the castle, and the waters sluiced into the hall through the narrow slit windows. After stillness had returned, a shadowy figure was cast up in the darkest corner of the hall.

'Ask him now,' said the younger brother. 'You don't have much time.'

'Has my wife been unfaithful to me?' asked the young husband.

'No. She has always been faithful. Why would you doubt it?'

Thunder rolled, lightning forked across the sky, the loch rose up again and threw water into the chamber, and the floor of the hall bucked and rattled. When peace returned, the dark figure was still there in the darkest corner.

'He won't leave empty-handed,' the younger brother said to the old woman. 'Who can you spare?'

The Lady of Ardvreck went to the door of the hall. She took the iron ring in her bony hand and twisted it. The latch squeaked up, the door swung wide, and there stood the servant girl, trembling with terror at the tumultuous events of the previous few minutes. The old woman pointed to the girl.

'Not her,' said the dark figure. 'Her soul is spotless.'

The waters of the lake rose up a third time. They swilled in through the windows and dashed people and furniture against the walls.

'Take the old woman,' said the younger brother.

'She's mine already; and it's not yet her time.' The water began to drain out of the hall. The dark figure spoke again. 'I will take someone whom your sister will miss much more.'

Outside, the sky lightened and the surface of the loch calmed. In the room there was no sign of the dark figure.

The three men made their way back to the home of the one who was married. They were relieved that they had survived unscathed, though both brothers wondered which of them would have to fight for his soul, and when. As they approached the house, they heard a wail which chilled them more than anything they had seen or heard in Ardvreck Castle that day. They ran towards the house. Out of the open door, and into the late afternoon sunshine, stepped the young wife, clutching the lifeless body of her unbaptised child.

For the next five years, the Assynt crops grew black and shrivelled, and there were no herring to be caught in the loch. Then the castle burnt down – though no one knows how the fire started – and the Lady of Ardvreck died in the flames. After that, the crops returned to their normal state, and the herring to the loch.

# WAIFS AND STRAYS

The following five stories are not tied to any particular location. I've included them because they are among my favourites, and also because of the different ways they contribute to the picture of stories and storytelling in the Highlands.

The first, The Story of Fergus Smith, is an oddity. A long time ago my youngest daughter heard me tell it. Years later she repeated it to me, when I had utterly forgotten it, and subsequently I began to tell it again. I've no idea where the story came from, though it is reminiscent of the Orkney tale of Assipattle and the Mester Stoor Worm (which is actually set in Caithness). It's an example of how stories can sometimes take on a life of their own.

The Three Advices is the title often given to a story which was popular among the older generation of Scottish Travellers. Although it's a powerful tale with ancient roots, it's not as widely known as it might be. This is my own telling, which draws on the version told by Alec Williamson. Alec himself is the source for The Wee Boy and the Minister, and the text given here is from his own words. It's one of Alec's favourite stories among the many he first heard in Gaelic from his father.

The Wren is my own version of a story I have heard Essie Stewart tell many times. Essie had it from her Traveller grandfather, the celebrated Gaelic storyteller who was known as Ailidh Dall – Blind Sandy Stewart.

The final story among the Waifs and Strays, Hogmanay at Hallowe'en, has variants recorded in so many places that I wanted to give the reader the opportunity to imagine it happening wherever he or she spotted a Sìthean – a fairy hill (and many are marked on maps). It's a classic tale of Highland fairy lore, incorporating in a short space many of the firmly held beliefs concerning the *daoine sìth* and their way of life: the Sìthean door is only open to mortals at certain times of the year; there always seems to be a party going on inside, with dancing and incomparable music; time in the mound runs much slower than time outside; and iron or steel (in this story, the tip of a gaff) have the power to protect against enchantment and fairy attacks.

In many versions of Hogmanay at Hallowe'en, the drink that the two men go out to find is whisky rather than brandy, a reminder that the Highlands were, until quite recently, famous or notorious for the vast number of illicit stills concealed in caves and on heathery slopes.

## ⁓ The Story of Fergus Smith ⁓

There was once a boy called Fergus, whose father was a smith. Fergus spent a lot of time in the smithy, and when anyone asked him what he wanted to do when he left school he would always say, 'I want to be a smith, like my dad.' This would annoy his father greatly because, although Fergus spent a lot of the time in the smithy, he spent it staring into the fire and dreaming – dreaming of adventures with princesses and dragons, and of mortal combat.

So one day Fergus' father said to him, 'Every time you're asked what you want to do when you leave school you say you want to be a smith, but I've never seen you do a hand's turn around this place. You just sit and stare into the fire all day, like a useless lump. I'm sick of it, so I'm going to set you a test. Tomorrow I've got some business to do in town, and I'm going to leave you here to look after the forge. All you have to do is keep the fire going, nothing else. In fact, don't try to do anything else. If I get back and the fire's still in, we'll see about training you up, but if the fire's out you're off to become an accountant or something equally useless.'

Next morning, Fergus' father left his son with instructions and went into town. Fergus couldn't see how there would be any problem, as long as he kept the fire topped up and gave an occasional pump on the bellows. He was sitting on the anvil, watching the sparks rise in the shapes of castles and mountain peaks, when an old man with a long white beard came in.

'Where's the hammer?' the old man asked Fergus.

Fergus had no idea. He looked around and spotted a big hammer in a corner. 'Over there. That must be it.'

The old man took the hammer and stood by the door. An old woman entered. The old man raised the hammer and brought it down on the old woman's head, and she dropped, dead as a stone. Fergus was amazed. The very day he'd been left in charge, and this had to happen. The old man was off out of the door, leaving behind the bloody hammer. It took Fergus a couple of minutes to collect his wits, then it became plain that he had to find his father.

It was a long and fruitless quest. Fergus did the rounds of the coal merchant, the station, the pubs, but no one had seen his dad. As he stood wondering where to try next, the old man came out of an alley with two of the King's guards. 'That's him,' he sobbed, pointing to Fergus. 'That's the thug who killed my poor wife.'

The guards grabbed Fergus and marched him to the palace, in through the great oak doors, up the marble staircase and into the King's chamber. Fergus looked at the King. He was a pitiful sight, for the poor man's head was covered in boils, and every so often one of them would burst with a soft pop.

'So,' said the King, 'what have you been up to?'

'I'm innocent of any crime, Your Majesty. But if you'll trust me and pardon me of the crime I didn't commit, I think I might be able to cure you of your affliction.'

'My boy, if you can cure me of my affliction, not only will I pardon you of the crime – whether you committed it or not – but I'll also give you half my kingdom and the hand of my daughter in marriage.'

Fergus' granny was a bit of a wise woman. He was very fond of

her, and had spent a lot of time in her kitchen, watching her pre-
pare potions. He remembered one in particular. Fergus pointed
out of the window. 'See those cows,' he said to the King's servants.
'I want you to go down and collect as much of their poo as you can.
It has to be warm, so preferably catch it before it touches the ground.'

The servants went out into the fields and returned after a while
with silver trays full and steaming. 'Now,' said Fergus, 'cover the
King's head with the poo.'

The servants looked doubtfully at the King, but the King
nodded, and they began to apply the poo in big handfuls until his
head was entirely covered – except for two little holes at the nostrils,
so that he could breathe.

'Now we must wait until it dries,' said Fergus. It took a long
time, but at last the King's head was covered in a solid brown crust.

'Peel off the poo,' said Fergus to the servants, 'and be very, very
gentle.' Gradually, in tiny pieces, the brown crust was removed.
When it was entirely off, everyone in the room, except Fergus,
gasped, for the King's head was now as smooth as a baby's bottom.
A mirror was held up for him. For a long time he just gaped, then
he smiled, began to hum a little tune and did a jiggy kind of a dance
on the spot.

'Your Majesty,' said Fergus, bowing low, 'I'm sure I don't have to
remind you of your promise.'

'Of course not, my boy. You're pardoned herewith and the hand
of the Princess and half the kingdom are yours. Though I should
tell you, there are a couple of small caveats.'

'Your Majesty?'

'The half of the kingdom that you've come into is under the sway
of a terrible fire-breathing dragon. The only thing that stops him
from laying waste to the other half of the kingdom is a regular diet
of sixteen-year-old girls. And the Princess is the only one of those
poor, innocent creatures left in the whole of the realm. I fear we
may need to sacrifice her soon.'

'Where is this dragon?' asked Fergus bravely. The King, still
admiring his new complexion, pointed vaguely out of the window
towards the east.

It took Fergus three days and nights of travelling to reach the
coast, and when he got there the sun was beginning to rise behind a
large hill to one side of a bay. As the sun got higher the hill seemed
to move, which Fergus thought must be a trick of the light – until

he realised that the hill had a tail which was slowly uncurling, and a head which swung dreamily towards him. Out of the head stared two huge, yellow eyes.

The dragon had awoken from its sleep, and was now fully unfurled. Smoke puffed from its nostrils as it headed in what was undoubtedly Fergus' direction. Fergus looked around. Behind him was the road that had brought him there. No escape in that direction. But to his side was the beach, and pulled up on the beach was a little boat. He ran to the boat, pushed it out into the water, took the oars and began to row.

The dragon had a mean look in its eyes. It had expected to find a sixteen-year-old girl waiting when it woke, and to find Fergus instead was both irritating and a disappointment. But breakfast was breakfast. The dragon veered from the road and onto the beach. At the sea's edge it put first one green, scaly foot, then another, into the water, until its whole body except the head was immersed; then it began to swim.

Fergus pulled as hard as he could on the oars, but the dragon was a mighty beast, and there was no question that it was gaining on the little boat. It stretched out its head, planning to take in a great breath of air before breathing out a single devastating flame that would nicely cook both the vessel and its occupant. But its head was too low down and, instead of air, it breathed in water.

As Fergus watched, the dragon's eyes started to bulge out of its head, steam came from its ears and nostrils, and its body swelled up like a balloon. There was a terrible bang, and Fergus woke. He opened his eyes and saw before him the cold ashes of the smithy fire. The bang was caused by his father coming in and slamming the door behind him in annoyance, as he realised that his son had failed utterly in the one simple task that had been set for him.

Next day Fergus' dad enrolled him on a basic accountancy course at the local college. He didn't stay long, though. He left college, set up in business, and made a fortune with a product that, until quite recently, was still displayed on the shelves of many chemists' shops. The label proclaimed:

From an old family recipe. Granny Smith's Patent Boil Remover. By Royal Appointment. Warning: for external application only. Under no circumstances drink contents!

# ⁓ The Three Advices ⁓

They were the hardest of times. A song that was doing the rounds told how the rich got the gravy and the poor got the blame.

There was a man called Iain who was a master tailor by trade, but no one wanted fine clothes any more, and he had no work. For a while he sat at home, while his wife, whose name was Annie, went out begging. Magnus, their eleven-year-old son, would go with her. He could play a couple of tunes on the penny whistle, and his talents encouraged the coppers and an occasional piece of silver to chink into the hat.

One day, after his wife and son had returned home, Iain said, 'You're making enough to keep you going here. I'm going to hit the road and look for work. There must be employment somewhere. Don't worry about me. I'll be back, but I don't know when.' He wasn't a very practical man, and Annie tried to discourage him from leaving, but he'd made up his mind. He put the tools of his trade in his pocket, and set off the next morning to seek his fortune.

Iain travelled a long way in his quest for work. In every town there were people reeling around from the effects of cheap drink; there were fights and muggings, and homeless souls wrapped in blankets out on the streets, too helpless to move. Whenever Iain came to a village he was driven off by the dogs, and for weeks he slept rough, eating what he could forage from the hedgerows and steal from the fields. One day he got himself to a hiring fair. One of the farmers seemed to take a fancy to him. 'You're a likely looking fellow. Do you have any special skills?' When Iain told the farmer that he was a tailor by trade, he seemed very satisfied, saying that there were always clothes needing mending around the farm, and that if Iain would be willing to do general farm work as well as tailoring, he would hire him for the year.

The farm was a good place to be employed. The farmer treated his workers fairly, and every day there was porridge for breakfast, bread and cheese and ale out in the fields, and a hearty stew round the kitchen table in the evening. The farmer's wife was a kind woman, though you had to stay on the right side of her, as she was known to possess the second sight, as well as other powers beyond the normal. For example, she could make milk sour in the jug, just by looking at it, and make a dead herring jump out of the cart.

After his first year on the farm, Iain hired up for a second without giving it a thought, and time passed so swiftly that a third year had gone before it occurred to him that he should think about getting back home. Of course there were no mobile phones – or phones of any kind – in those days, and he wasn't much of a writer, so it hadn't occurred to him to try and send a letter to his family. As I said, he wasn't a very practical man.

So Iain went to the farmer and told him he thought it was time for him to return to his family.

'Your family?'

'I've got a wife and son, Annie and Magnus.'

'You should have told me. I had no idea. You've been away a long time. I hope they're still waiting for you.'

'Oh they'll be waiting. I told them I'd be back and that I didn't know when.'

'Well, good luck to you. We shall miss you. You've been a good worker. My wife will sort you out in the morning before you leave.'

Next morning, Iain said goodbye to his fellow workers and went to the kitchen. The farmer's wife sat at the table, and there was a loaf of bread in front of her. Iain could smell that it was fresh out of the oven.

'Now Iain,' said the farmer's wife, 'I'm going to give you a choice, and think hard before you decide. The choice is this: you can either have your wages, or three pieces of advice.'

Iain did think hard. His wages must amount to a good sum; though, not being a very practical man, he had no idea how much. But three pieces of advice from this wise woman could go a long way, and he knew that she didn't make that kind of offer to everyone. So it was the advice he decided to take.

'Very well. The first piece of advice is never to take the short cut. The second is, never spend the night in a house where there's a young, red-haired woman, and an old man. And the third piece of advice – never strike a blow in anger without counting to ten first. Now take this loaf of bread, and when you get home break it, and give half to your wife and the other half to your son.'

Iain thanked her, took the loaf, and set off down the road. He met three pedlars going the same way, and started to walk along with them. Iain asked them how things had been in the world for the past three years, and they told him that life was not as bad as it used to be, and that more people were buying from them than in the worst times. The pedlars were good fun, full of jokes and riddles and songs, and their company made the time pass quickly. It began to grow dark. They were up on a barren heath, a good way from the town, when they reached a fork in the road.

'Here's the short cut,' said the pedlars. 'It'll get us to the town that much quicker.' Iain remembered the first piece of advice, and told them he thought he would prefer to go the long way.

'Suit yourself,' said the pedlars, 'see you at the inn. We'll get the drinks in.' And they set off down the short cut, singing the song that begins 'As I cam' o'er the Muir of Ord…' Iain hadn't gone far along the main route when he heard yells and cries of pain coming from behind him, and he hurried on a little faster than he might otherwise have done.

When he got to the outskirts of the town a sliver of moon was hanging just above the roofs of the houses. Three figures staggered towards him out of the darkness. It was the pedlars, battered and bruised. On their way through the short cut they had been set upon by thieves, robbed of all they possessed, and given a good kicking into the bargain. Iain took them in hand. 'I'm sure,' he said, 'we can call on someone's charity and find shelter for the night.'

They were turned away many times until at last they were at the far end of the town and going back into the countryside, when they came to a big house, set by itself. Iain knocked at the door and they waited. At last the door was opened by a young woman, who had a rich head of red hair.

'There's four of us,' said Iain. 'Would you be able to give us shelter for the night? We can do work for you in the morning.'

'Of course,' said the young, red-haired woman. 'You're very welcome. Come in and I'll find you a bite to eat before you go to bed.' There was a sound from inside, a hacking cough. Iain looked past the woman, and saw an old man sitting in a high-backed chair, spitting into a handkerchief. He remembered the second piece of advice and turned to his companions, the pedlars. 'Boys, I reckon we should maybe find somewhere else to stay.' But the pedlars were exhausted and they couldn't believe their luck. They were across the threshold before Iain had finished speaking. The door closed, and Iain was left out in the cold and the dark. There was a barn close to the house, so he made himself comfortable and warm among the hay, and went to sleep.

Some time during the night, Iain was woken by voices talking in whispers. He made a porthole in the hay and looked out, and there was the young, red-haired woman talking to a handsome man who was wrapped about in a magnificent tartan cloak.

'It's a perfect night for it,' said the woman. 'You can do the deed and those pedlars will get the blame. Then we won't have to hide our love any longer.'

The handsome man and young, red-haired woman started to kiss and canoodle, and while they were lost in the heat of their passion, Iain took his tailor's scissors from his pocket, reached out, and cut a small square of cloth from the man's tartan cloak. Next morning he lay still among the hay, waiting until the fake screams from the woman had subsided, and the pedlars had been taken away to be tried and condemned for murdering the old man. During the day, Iain managed to find a couple of hen's eggs to crack and to eat raw. He spent the next night in the barn and left for town early in the morning.

There was a big crowd gathered in the town square, and lots of excitement in anticipation of the hanging of the three miserable-looking pedlars, who stood shivering on the scaffold. Iain was astonished to see the handsome man in the tartan cloak climb the ladder, stand beside them, and begin to read out the sentence. He was plainly the magistrate who had condemned them.

A big, stout man stood at the side of the scaffold. His head was shaven and he wore a gun in a holster, and Iain was sure he must be the chief of police. Iain went up to the man and spoke deferentially, told him the story of the conversation in the barn, and showed him the little square of tartan. The chief of police stopped the hanging just as the nooses were being placed around the three pedlars' necks, and it wasn't long before the magistrate himself was dangling from a rope, while his lover was taken off to be burnt in a tar barrel.

Iain decided that it would be best to leave that town before anything else dramatic occurred, so he went out through the gates and set off for home. After three days he arrived at his house, early in the morning of a bright spring day. The house looked well cared for. The garden was neat and in one corner there were rows of vegetables beginning to sprout. The front door was painted red, and Iain was sure it had been green when he left three years before.

The door was unbolted. He opened it and stepped into the hall, tiptoed up the stairs – remembering to miss out the one that always creaked – and went along the corridor. The bedroom door was ajar.

Iain prodded it with a finger and it swung open. His wife, Annie, lay in the bed, and by her side was a handsome young man. Both were sound asleep. Iain stepped forward and raised his fists as tears rolled down his cheeks, and then he remembered the third piece of advice given to him by the farmer's wife – never strike a blow in anger without counting to ten first.

Iain had reached nine when Annie opened her eyes. 'Good grief!' she said, 'It's you! I thought we'd never see you again.' She shook the handsome young man lying next to her. 'Magnus, wake up! Look who's here. Your father's come back at last.'

So there was a great reunion, and Iain learned that, during the time he had been away, Magnus' penny whistle playing had improved so much that he was now a respected and well-paid professional, in great demand for weddings and dances. He told his wife and son about his adventures, the farm and the pedlars, and the whispering in the barn, and how he had been saved by the three pieces of advice given to him by the farmer's wife.

Iain reached into his pack. 'I almost forgot,' he said, taking out the loaf. 'When I got back home I was to break it in two, and give you each a half.' He broke open the bread, and out fell his wages.

This is a story about a wee boy. He was a schoolboy, but he was never at school. He was guilty of truancy, and he never went to school. Well, his parents were sending him, but he would be away fishing or guddling or whatever.

So this day he was up a burn fishing, and along comes a minister – the village minister. He was taking a walk, and he saw the wee boy, and he said, 'You're at your usual,' he said, 'you're not in school.'

'No,' he said, 'I'm not in school. I don't like school.'

'And what are you going to be when you leave school?' said the minister. 'If you don't go to school, how are you going to read? How are you going to write?'

'Ach,' he said, 'I'll manage, I will manage.'

So the minister looked in the heather and he grabbed a horseshoe, and he said, 'What is that, tell me what is that?'

'I have no idea what that is.'

'You've no idea?'

'I don't know what it is,' he said.

'Well,' the minister said, 'that is a horseshoe.'

'Now,' said the boy, 'I can see the point in schooling and education. You knew it was a horseshoe didn't you?'

The minister said, 'Yes, anybody would.'

'Now me, you see, I wouldna know but that would be a mare's shoe.'

'Ah well,' the minister said.

'Ah, but you said you knew it was a horseshoe. So,' he said, 'you didn't know, did you?'

So the minister said, 'You're not as green as you're cabbage looking.' And he said to the wee boy, 'Where do you stay?'

'On the other side of the village,' said the boy. 'A remote part.'

'Is your house on the right-hand side, or the left-hand side of the road?'

'Well,' he said, 'it's sometimes on the right-hand side, sometimes on the left-hand side. And,' he said, 'it's thatched on one side.'

'Thatched on one side? Very queer house,' the minister said. 'I see. And,' he said, 'who's in the house with you?'

'My father, my mother, my brother, my sister.'

'Right then,' he said, 'what was your sister doing when you left the day?'

'My sister was crying,' he said.

'Crying?' said the minister. 'I'm very sorry to hear it. Why was she crying?'

'She was crying,' he said, 'the laughing that she did last year.'

'Very peculiar. And your father,' he said, 'what was your father doing?'

'My father was very busy. He was grinding the meal.'

'Grinding the meal?'

'Aye,' said the boy, 'he was grinding the meal. He was grinding the meal that we ate last year.'

'Oh, good God. And your mother – what's your mother do?'

'Ah, my mother canna do an awful lot. She's on one hand. She has only the use of one hand.'

'Oh, I'm sorry to hear that,' said the minister.

'Aye, you don't need to be.'

'And your brother. What's your brother do?'

'My brother,' he said, 'he's up on the hill. He's hunting. And the game that he's killing, he's leaving them. And them that he's not getting, he's taking them home.

'Oh for goodness' sake. That's very peculiar, that,' said the minister.

'Yes,' he said, 'it is, but it's true.'

Well the minister said, I think he said, 'You are quite a smart fellow. So I am going to give you a little test now,' he said.

'What test is that?'

'Tomorrow – you have a wee brother?'

'Aye, a wee brother. He's about four year old.'

'Well,' said the minister, 'tomorrow you'll take that brother to me, and he won't be on the road, and he'll not be off the road. There'll no be any clothes on him, and there'll no be clothes off him. And,' he said, 'his face won't be towards me, and his back won't be towards me. Can you manage it?'

'Aye, I think I can manage it.'

So the boy went home, and he said to the wee brother in the morning, 'Come on, get up. You've a job to do,' he said.

'What are you going to do?' said the wee brother.

'Come on with me,' he said. 'Don't put any clothes on.' So he took him into a shed, and he put a piece of a herring net on him. And he went to the pigsty, and lo and behold he takes a big sow from it.

'Now,' he said, 'lie on your stomach, across her back, longways.'

Now, I don't know if you know how stubborn a pig can be. If you were taking a pig and you wanted to get her to Dingwall, you'd better put her to Perth because she'll turn anyway, so she's a stubborn animal. And she was off the road and on the road, off the road and on the road.

And the minister met them. 'That'll do,' he said, 'that'll do. You done it,' he said.

'Well,' said the boy, 'look, he's not facing you, is he?'

'No,' said the minister. 'It's the crown that's facing towards me.'

'Yep. And there's no clothes on him.'

'No,' said the minister.

'But there's no clothes off him, he has a herring net.'

'Yes, you're very good – you're brilliant. But I didna get on so well with your little testers. So now you'll tell me now aboot this. Your father, for instance. How is he grinding the meal that you ate last year?'

'Well, last year was a poor, poor year – a poor crop. We had to borrow. Now we're paying it back, so therefore he's grinding the meal that we ate last year.

'And what aboot your sister, crying the laughing that she did?'

'Well last year,' the boy said, 'she was going to dances, she was going to concerts, she had boyfriends. This year,' he says, 'she has a wee baby and she canna get oot the bloody house. So of course she's crying – she's crying the laughing she did last year.'

'Oh aye,' said the minister, 'true, true. Oh the little harlot,' he said. 'And what about your mother with one hand?'

'My mother has the one hand – she has a baby in the other hasn't she?'

'Oh I see, I see. And your house now. How can it be on the right-hand side, and on the left-hand side?'

'Well it depends which direction you're coming from.'

'And how it is only thatched on one side?'

'It's thatched on the outside.'

'OK then, we'll go to the hunter, your brother. How is he leaving them that he's killing, and taking them that he's not finding – taking them home?'

'My brother,' said the boy, 'he's very unhygienic, you know? He's a dirty bugger. He never washes, and he got lousy. So he's up on the hill, and he has his shirt off. And he's taking the wee beasts from the shirt and throwing them away. And them that he's no' finding, he's taking them home, isn't he?'

'Yes he is,' says the minister. He said, 'You're good, right enough, whether you go to school or not, you're brilliant. And I think,' he said, 'you're quite a little wit.'

Well I think that's what the minister said.

## ~ The Wren ~

One winter night, in the middle of a blizzard, a little wren was looking for shelter. It came to a field full of sheep. The sheep refused to help, all but one, who told the wren to climb onto her back. The wren fell asleep in the sheep's wool. When it woke in the morning, it knew something was wrong. All the warmth had gone.

The wren fluttered out into the open, and saw that the sheep was dead. Its throat had been torn out by a wolf. The wren was determined to have revenge. It flew to a field where a farmer was working, and perched on his shoulder.

'If you help me kill the wolf that killed my friend, I'll tell you where there's a keg of brandy.'

'Done,' said the farmer. 'First, the brandy. Where is it?'

'Down on the beach. But you'll need to take your horse and cart. It's a big barrel.'

The farmer set off for the beach, driving his horse, with the wren fluttering behind. He managed to heave the barrel – it was a big one – onto the cart.

'Now let's go and find that wolf,' said the wren.

'Push off,' said the farmer. 'I've got what I wanted. I'm going home to enjoy myself.'

'You'll regret that,' said the wren, 'because now you can say good-bye to your brandy.'

The wren landed on the barrel and began to peck at it. The farmer was furious. He took an axe from the back of the cart and swung at the wren. The wren flew up, and the farmer hit the barrel. It split open, and the brandy gushed away into the sand.

'Now I'm going to kill your horse.'

The wren landed on the horse's head and started to peck. Another swing of the axe, and the horse lay dead with its skull split open.

'Now say goodbye to your cart.'

The little bird hopped about on the cart, pecking away, and soon the axe blows reduced the cart to matchwood.

'Your turn next.'

Finally the wren came to land on the farmer's shin, still pecking. A last swing and the farmer lay on the brandy-soaked beach, his leg broken, amid the ruins of the cart, and next to the corpse of his horse. Night came before his servants found him and carried him home.

Meanwhile the wren had headed back in the direction of the farm. In a field it saw the farmer's cows and his bull.

'See that barn,' said the wren to the bull. 'It's full of good things to eat. You and your wives could have a real feast in there.'

'But we're penned in the field. We can't get through the gate.'

'Nonsense! A strong fellow like you could lift that gate up with his horns, no bother at all.'

That had never occurred to the bull. He lifted up the gate, and he and the cows ambled into the barn where they ate so much that they burst. And that was the end of the farmer's cattle.

The wren caught sight of a starving sheepdog that had just had pups, and flew down to speak to her.

'You look hungry. I know where you can find a good supply of fresh meat, just what you need to keep you strong while you're feeding your little ones. All you have to do is help me kill the wolf that killed my friend.'

The dog agreed, so the two of them set off for the wolf's den. 'Wait outside,' said the wren when they got there. 'The wolf will be out shortly.'

Inside the den the wren found the wolf dozing in a corner. 'Lots of good food out there,' it whispered in his ear.

'I dare say there is,' grunted the wolf.

'No, really good food. You'd be foolish to miss the chance.'

'Oh come on, then,' said the wolf. As soon as he was out in the open the sheepdog flew at him. The fight was soon over, and the wolf lay dead.

'Now,' said the wren, 'if you go down to the barn you'll find plenty of fresh beef. Enjoy the feast.'

Night had fallen, and the wren was looking for somewhere to rest. Passing by the farmhouse it saw a light in the upstairs window, and flew over to see what was going on. The window was open a crack, and the wren squeezed through. The farmer lay in bed, with his leg in plaster and a big stick by his side to help him get around. When he saw the wren he grabbed it and held it tight. 'I'm going to take your head off with my thumb,' he said.

But the wren pooped in the farmer's hand and he let it go. It landed on the photograph of the farmer's adored late mother and began to peck at the frame. The farmer lifted his stick and swung; the wren flew up, and the picture was smashed. Round the room went the wren, and, in its wake, splinters of glass and wood, and shards of pottery, filled the air.

'Let that be a lesson to you,' said the wren to the farmer. 'Now you've lost everything, and all because you wouldn't do a good turn for a little wren.'

The farmer lay weeping among the wreckage of his most precious possessions, and the wren flew off into the night.

There were two men, and they were returning home one Hogmanay evening after buying a keg of brandy for the celebrations later that night. One of them had the keg on his shoulder, and they were looking forward to sampling the contents. They were coming back up the glen, when from away up the hill they heard the sound of the pipes. They looked and there was a light in the distance.

The man with the keg on his shoulder was a piper himself, and he thought that he'd never heard such wonderful playing. So he began to climb the hill towards the light, and his companion followed him. As they got closer, they realised that the light was coming from an open door in a Sìthean – a fairy hill. They crept up and peered in. Inside was a huge room, full of light, with tables bending under the weight of the food and drink, and beautiful people dancing.

The man with the keg leapt into the Sìthean, linked arms with one of the dancers, and began to birl around the room. Before his friend could get in there, the door slammed shut, and he was left out in the darkness on the cold hillside.

What could he do but go down to the village and tell everyone what had happened? And of course they didn't believe him. He was taken to Inverness and brought up before the sheriff for murder – but there was no body, no evidence against him, so he was set free.

When he got back home everyone shunned him. But in time, because he led a decent life, he became accepted once more, and things gradually got back to normal.

Well, it was the following Hallowe'en. He'd been out fishing for trout, and he had with him a gaff with a steel hook on the end. It was getting dark and, as he was coming up through the glen, he heard the sound of the pipes in the distance. He realised it was the place where he and his friend had heard the pipes the previous Hogmanay. He looked up, and there was a distant light. The door to the Sìthean was open again.

He climbed up through the trees until he got to the entrance of the Sìthean, and peered in. There was the room, full of light,

and the tables with the food and drink, and the beautiful people. And there, dancing among them, with the keg of brandy still on his back, was his friend. He jammed the gaff in the open door and when his friend danced close by he reached in, grabbed him by the elbow, and pulled him out. Then he pulled out the gaff and the door of the Sìthean slammed shut. And the two of them were in the darkness, on the cold hillside.

As they were going down to the village, the one with the keg on his shoulder said that he thought he'd only been in the mound for a few hours – and there he was, ten months later!

When they got back home, people were so pleased to see them that they broke open the keg of brandy, and that year they celebrated Hogmanay at Hallowe'en.

# STORIES IN STONE

Strathpeffer is a village in Mid Ross. Long ago it became celebrated for the curative powers of its waters, and people travelled long distances to take them. By 1885, the village's reputation as a spa was so widespread that a branch railway line was extended from the nearby town of Dingwall. At the same time, the local landowners created the hotels, including the massive Highland and the Ben Wyvis, which range up the steep sides of the strath; and they built boarding houses which were then rented to private landladies – all to accommodate a great influx of visitors, among whom were Robert Louis Stevenson, Florence Nightingale and George Bernard Shaw.

No one comes to Strathpeffer to take the waters any more, which in any case are foul and sulphurous, but in the summer it's a popular overnight stop for coach parties. Visitors from all over the world are charmed by the Spa Gardens and the splendid, glass-clad Pavilion which was once the foremost music venue for this part of the Highlands (The Beatles very nearly played there).

Mairi and I live above Strathpeffer in a small community called
Ardival, halfway up a hill below the ridge that is known as the Cat's
Back. Until quite recently Ardival – from the Gaelic, meaning the
township, or maybe just the farmstead, on the heights – was a scat-
tering of houses among woodland. It now consists mainly of quite
large modern houses, and our 1930s bungalow nestles among them.

Shortly after we moved in we spent an evening with the great
Aberdeen storyteller and ballad singer, the late Stanley Robertson,
listening to the songs and memories of his north-east Traveller
family, and being bamboozled by his fortune-telling skills – 'just for
fun', as Stanley was a member of the Mormon Church. He was also
very sensitive to the presence of spirits in a place. Next morning,
over breakfast, he told me: 'I didn't want to say anything last night,
but the whole time we were talking, there was a Highland chieftain
standing behind you. He was wearing the full Highland regalia, he
had a big beard, and he wants you to do something for him.'

On the occasions when I met Stanley after this, he would still
be pondering the details of the mission. Though we never discovered what the chieftain wanted me to do, Stanley did say that he
used to be a visitor to the cottage, and we decided that he may
have had a lady friend here. This is by way of saying that Ardival is
not necessarily the tranquil rural spot it seems to be at first sight, a
judgement which is confirmed by the existence of the Ardival cats.
As I'm typing, there's a movement beyond the window. Along the
top of the wall walks a black cat with white paws and a white bib.
I've never seen this animal before. He or she is one of the many
cats who visit the community, stalk through the gardens and lurk
among the bushes. No one is quite sure where they come from, or
where they've gone to when we realise that it's a while since they
were last seen.

Our next-door neighbours, Stuart and Heather, are very fond
of cats. If one of these semi-feral beasts wanders into their garden,
they will put down food to entice it into the shed at the side of their

house. When the animal gets used to them they will start to groom it, and perhaps take it to the vet for necessary injections. They are kind people.

A couple of years ago a cat, a male tabby, strayed into the Ardival community. We watched him as he wandered about, coat matted with mud and bristling with twigs, a weeping eye, and an ear which may have been chewed in a fight. Heather and Stuart took him in, cleaned him up, and got him to the vet. He was transformed into a sleek being whose coat had a hint of the Persian, and whose tail stood up proudly like a cloud of exotic smoke. They called him Harry, after the Clint Eastwood cop, remembering the fact that he once had been very dirty.

Harry became the Laird of Ardival. He went from house to house, never settling down in any one place – and we had no notion where he spent his nights – but graciously accepting food wherever it was offered. You always knew Harry was at the door because he summoned you with a high-pitched squeak, for at some point during his life he had lost his miaow. When you opened the door, Harry would pause at the threshold, peering into the house as if, perhaps, he dimly remembered being terrorised by an unruly toddler or a thoughtless dog in just such a place. When he was sure all was safe, he would step inside, perhaps eat some chicken or a little poached salmon, then lie down and roll over to present his tummy, as if he wanted to be stroked. To attempt to do this was, as cat owners will know, a big mistake. As soon as your fingers touched even the fur on Harry's belly, he would sink his claws into the hand that bore those fingers. That was Harry. He came into Ardival in early spring, and was a well-kent resident by mid-summer.

Some time in early autumn I was sitting in the kitchen, working at the laptop and looking out through the window across the strath to Ben Wyvis. Up in the woods above Ardival there's a maze, which the geologist and musician Helen Rowson had designed to be constructed from rocks brought there from all over the Highlands.

Mairi had gone up for some peace and quiet. It was early evening and the sun was going down, and I was thinking what a beautiful place this was to live, when I heard a high-pitched squeak. I opened the kitchen door and Harry was there, his two front paws up on the step. He peered inside, satisfied himself that there was no immediate danger, and stepped in. Turning up his nose at the food I offered, he lay on the rug and rolled over on his back to show me his tummy.

I went back to my typing. Outside, the light was fading, with just a dusting of orange sun on the very top western edge of the Ben. I heard the door open and close, Mairi coming back from her walk to the maze. When she came into the kitchen I could see that something was bothering her. She sat down, I made her a cup of tea, and then she began to tell her story.

'I was up at the maze and it was very peaceful and quiet, and getting quite dark up there. There were no birds singing and I couldn't hear any traffic sounds from down on the road. But then I did hear something. It sounded like voices way off in the wood. There was something spooky about it, so I hid behind one of the stones in the maze and waited. The voices seemed to be getting closer. I peeped out from behind the stone to see who it was, and what I saw was a group of little figures in a procession just at the edge of the woods, coming into the clearing. As they got closer I could see that they were cats. They were walking on their hind legs and carrying something on their shoulders. They got closer still, and I realised that what they were carrying was a cat-shaped coffin, and they were wailing, "Timmy Tomkins is dead! Timmy Tomkins is dead!" '

When Mairi said this, Harry rolled over, stood up on his back legs, beat his chest and said in a loud voice, 'Well, if Timmy Tomkins is dead, then I'm the King of the Cats!'

He went up the chimney with a great Whoosh, and we never saw him again.

# ～ FINN MACCOOL ～
## AND THE FINGALIANS OF KNOCK FARRIL

A track leads up from the maze, through forestry woodland, and out to the Cat's Back Ridge. Immediately below the Cat's Back, to the south, is Loch Ussie, and beyond the loch is the Brahan Estate. It's on this estate that Kenneth Mackenzie, who became known as the Brahan Seer, was employed. Legend has it that he was born in Lewis in the seventeenth century, but landed in this part of Ross-shire, where he came into possession of a magic stone. Through a hole in the stone he could both see into the future and also see what was happening in far-off places. These talents brought him no happiness, and he ended his life being burnt in a tar barrel at Chanonry Point in Fortrose. Before he died, though, he threw his stone into Loch Ussie, where it will remain until it is found by 'a lame humpbacked mendicant'.

The Cat's Back dips down and then rises up to Knock Farril hill. On the top of this hill are the remains of a fort, which archaeologists say dates back to the Iron Age. There's little left of it today, nothing more than traces of the foundations of the walls, but the stones that survive are remarkable in that they have been fused together by intense heat. More remarkable still, modern science has been unable to replicate the process that produced this vitrification.

There are a number of theories as to why the stones of this and other similar forts were melted together: it's possible that a timber structure within the walls caught fire accidentally, or perhaps was set alight during a battle; or the stones were deliberately fired to strengthen them; or perhaps the fort was built purely to display the power of the builder, a local bigwig, who then ordered it to be burnt down without it ever having been used.

A Strathpeffer legend tells a different story again. It says that, a long time ago, before people came to live in the Strath, there were giants in Knock Farril fort. These were the Irish hero Finn MacCool and his warriors, who lived there happily with their wives and children.

There was nothing Finn and his men enjoyed more than to go hunting through the Black Isle, off to the east, and to wade over the sea at the mouth of the Cromarty Firth to bring down the stags on Nigg Hill. One bright spring morning, they set off early, accompanied by the joyful blasts of Finn's horn, and with his great hunting dogs Bran and Sceolan straining at the leash ahead of them.

One of the band was late setting off. His name was Garry and, for a giant, he was short, just 15ft tall. Garry tried to catch up with the rest of the men, but couldn't, so eventually he gave up and trudged back to the fort. The women and children were waiting for him. They began to tease him, not just because he was short, but because he was ugly, and because his hair had never been cut or combed, and fanned out around his head like the leaves of a cabbage.

Garry was furious. He chased the women and children round and round the fort, but they outran him. At last, exhausted, he lay down and fell asleep. While he slept, the women took sharp wooden stakes and used them to pin his hair to the ground. When he woke they were leaning over him, still mocking. He tried to raise his head. At first he couldn't move it at all. He tried a second time and broke free, though his hair was ripped out at the roots. With blood spraying from his scalp, he chased the women and children into the fort, and barred the door with a great beam.

Garry began to pull up trees by their roots and stack them round the outside of the fort (which is why, if you go up there today, you'll find there are no trees on the top of Knock Farril). Then he took out his fire-making gear, the flint and the steel, and struck a spark into a handful of dried moss, holding the moss in the palm of his hand and blowing gently until it began to smoulder. Finally a tiny flame appeared. Still blowing, Garry knelt and laid the moss down on the ground and made a criss-cross of twigs over it. The twigs caught the flame which spread to the trees, and it wasn't long before the whole of the fort was encased in fire.

Way over to the east, on Nigg Hill, Finn MacCool and his warriors saw the column of smoke rising from the top of Knock Farril. They hurried back home, vaulting from bank to bank of the Cromarty Firth on their huge spears, but when they reached the fort it was too late. It had burned down to the ground, the stones had melted together, and all that was left of the women and children were little piles of white ash.

The story has two endings, and I don't know which one is true. The first account says that Garry fled, but was tracked down by Finn and his men to an unnamed glen, where they tore him to pieces; and that was how Glengarry got its name.

The other ending is quite different. It says that Garry was appalled by what he had done, and knew that he couldn't escape Finn's wrath. When the warriors arrived back at the fort he was still there, meekly awaiting his fate. He asked only that Finn himself should be his executioner.

Finn sat on a stone, took Garry by the hair, and placed the little giant's head over his knee. Then he unsheathed his sword – a magic sword called Mac an Lúin, which would cut through anything in one blow. Finn brought Mac an Lúin down on Garry's neck. The severed head rolled down the hill and came to rest in the valley bottom where, over time, it turned to stone, a great boulder which can still be seen today.

But Mac an Lúin had done the job too well. Not only had it removed Garry's head, it had cut deep into Finn's thigh. The warriors watched horrified. They had lost their women and children, and now their leader was in danger of bleeding to death. They lifted Finn on their shoulders, and began to make their way back to the Black Isle, with Bran and Sceolan trotting silently beside them.

The solemn procession came to Munlochy beach, and continued along the south shore until it reached the headland, where there's a cave. The warriors entered and gently laid Finn down on the cave floor, with his horn at his side. The dogs too lay down, and rested their chins on their paws, and the warriors stretched out on the floor. Dogs and men closed their eyes and fell into a deep sleep.

Many years later a shepherd was down on the beach, looking for a lost sheep. He found the cave entrance and went in, thinking that the sheep might be there. When his eyes got used to the gloom, he saw giant men and giant dogs, all sound asleep, and on the floor a giant horn.

A voice whispered in the shepherd's head, urging him to blow the horn. He picked it up, placed it to his lips and blew. Slowly the dogs began to lift their heads and, with a terrible creak of rusty old armour, the giant men raised themselves up on their elbows.

'Blow the horn again,' said the voice, and a second time the shepherd blew. The giant men and the giant dogs turned their heads towards the shepherd, opened their eyes and glared at him. The voice in his head told him to blow the horn a third time, but he lost his nerve, threw it back down on the floor, and headed towards the chink of light at the cave's entrance. Just as he was about to come out into the early morning sun, a chorus of sepulchral, groaning voices came out of the darkness: 'You fool, you've left us worse than you found us.'

The shepherd should have blown the horn three times, but he had only blown it twice. If he'd blown one more time, Finn MacCool, his men and the dogs, would have come fully back to life. As it was, they could see, they could hear, they could think, they could even speak a little, but they couldn't move their limbs; and still they wait for someone to find the cave and blow a third blast on the horn.

# MILLER'S WORLD
# OF WONDERS

Cromarty is best known today for its place in the litany of the BBC shipping forecast, sandwiched between Forties and Forth. The town to which the name belongs was once a Royal Borough. It's at the easternmost tip of the Black Isle, which itself is the most easterly part of Ross-shire. The Black Isle is not an island at all, but a peninsula that faces Inverness and the Moray coastline to the south, with the Nigg peninsula to the north across a narrow stretch of water. No one is sure how the Black Isle got its name. Some say it's because the soil there is rich and dark, but others insist that it once housed the greatest concentration of witches in the whole of the Highlands.

Thirty years ago Cromarty was quite an isolated place, unless you came to it by boat. When the Kessock Bridge opened in 1982 – spanning the Moray Firth, where a ferry had previously crossed – the town became much more accessible. Today it's within easy commuting distance of Inverness, is a thriving colony for artists, and caters for visitors, with teashops, dolphin-watching cruises and museums.

In his 1853 autobiography *My Schools and Schoolmasters*, Hugh Miller recalled a different Cromarty, which he watched from the windows of his school-house by the sea shore, in the early years of the nineteenth century:

> All the herring boats during the season passed our windows on their homeward way to the harbour; and, from their depth in the water, we became skilful enough to predicate the crans aboard of each with wonderful judgment and correctness. In days of good general fishings, too, when the curing-yards proved too small to accommodate the quantities brought ashore, the fish used to be laid in glittering heaps opposite the school-house door; and an exciting scene, that combined the

bustle of the workshop with the confusion of the crowded fair, would straightway spring up within twenty yards of the forms at which we sat, greatly to our enjoyment, and, of course, not a little to our instruction. We could see, simply by peering over book or slate, the curers going about rousing their fish with salt, to counteract the effects of the dog-day sun; bevies of young women employed as gutters, and horribly incarnadined with blood and viscera, squatting around in heaps, knife in hand, and plying with busy fingers their well-paid labours, at the rate of sixpence per hour; relays of heavily-laden fish-wives bringing ever and anon fresh heaps of herrings in their creels; and outside of all, the coopers hammering as if for life and death – now tightening hoops, and anon caulking with bulrush the leaky seams.

Hugh Miller was born in Cromarty in 1802. At that time, the town was a thriving fishing and trading port and Hugh's father was a relatively prosperous ship's captain who owned his own boat. But when Hugh was barely five years old, his father was lost in a storm on the way from Peterhead to Leith, together with his ship which was loaded with kelp, and the whole of the crew.

Late on a November afternoon in 1807, shortly before the news of his father's disappearance reached the Miller household, and just after the receipt of a reassuring letter from Peterhead, Hugh was sitting at his mother's side by the fire when the door of the cottage blew open. The little boy was sent to shut it, and saw in the gloom, 'as plainly as ever I saw anything', a detached hand and arm stretching out towards him. 'Hand and arm were apparently those of a female; they bore a livid and sodden appearance; and directly fronting me, where the body aught to have been, there was only blank, transparent space, through which I could see the dim forms of the objects beyond.'

Hugh was terrified and ran screaming to his mother. A servant was sent to perform the errand, and she too was startled by the same vision; but when Mrs Miller went to the door, there was no sign of the apparition.

In another early encounter with the supernatural, Hugh had been playing at the foot of the stairs when he saw, on the landing above him, 'a large, tall, very old man, attired in a light-blue greatcoat', whom he knew instinctively to be his buccaneering great-grandfather John Feddes. The cottage had been built for old John, dead many a year. Today it is a National Trust for Scotland property, whitewashed and immaculately thatched, and reputedly still haunted.

Though he loved reading, Hugh Miller performed poorly at school, preferring to explore the beaches, cliffs, caves and woods around Cromarty. He enjoyed the company of older folk, in particular that of his two uncles, James and Sandy Wright, who encouraged his natural curiosities, which included an interest in the fossils found in the rocks around Cromarty. This enthusiasm developed into a life-long preoccupation which has seen Miller become recognised as an important pioneer in the study of geology.

Another pleasure when he was a boy was to visit his cousins in Lairg, a 30-mile journey to the north-west, which Hugh and his mother would make together on foot. Hardly any Gaelic was spoken in Cromarty, or in the house, though his mother Harriet, descended from a legendary elder with the second sight, was fluent. But up in Sutherland it was the everyday language. The house was: '...a low, long, dingy edifice of turf, four or five rooms in length, but only one in height, that, lying along a gentle acclivity, somewhat resembled at a distance a huge black snail creeping up a hill.' The family sitting-room, in traditional style, had an open fire in the middle, with no chimney, and folk sat around it '...in a wide circle – the women invariably ranged on the one side, and the men on the other'. Elderly men from the neighbourhood would gather round this fire, and young Hugh listened to narratives of clan feuds, and to some of the old stories that had come over from Ireland centuries before, 'wild Fingalian legends'. By his side, his cousin George translated in a whisper. The stories included the tale of Diarmuid, who eloped with Grainne, Finn MacCool's betrothed, and was poisoned by the spine of a giant boar; another story of Finn, told around the peat fire in Lairg, was the legend of Knock Farril.

When he was fifteen years old, young Hugh's formal education finished abruptly, after a fight with his schoolmaster. He became an apprentice stonemason, encouraged by the fact that his cousin George in Lairg, who was himself a mason, had little to do during the winter months. This seasonal leisure gave Hugh the opportunity to pursue his explorations of beach and quarry, and his literary interests. But in his autobiography, he bears graphic witness to the harshness of his trade, describing from first-hand the gruelling work in Gairloch in Wester Ross, and then in Edinburgh. It broadened his experience of the world, but breathing in the dust from the stone infected his lungs. He returned to Cromarty and began to find some success writing pieces for the *Inverness Courier*. Then, in 1831, he met and fell in love with nineteen-year-old Lydia Fraser. Her mother disapproved of their courtship because of his apparently poor prospects, until he gained a post as an accountant for the recently opened Cromarty branch of the Commercial Bank.

By the time he and Lydia married in 1837, Hugh had published his first book, *Scenes and Legends of the North of Scotland*. By the time of his death (by his own hand) on Christmas Eve 1856, he had become the editor of *The Witness*, a twice-weekly Edinburgh newspaper which championed the cause of the Free Church, but also achieved a general readership second only to that of *The Scotsman*. He worked tirelessly as a campaigner, a touring lecturer, and a writer. His geological books were instant bestsellers in his lifetime, and for many decades thereafter. No one knows why he ended his life with a pistol shot to the chest, but it seems likely that ill-health, overwork and what, today, we would call depression, all had a part to play.

One of Hugh Miller's most popular books, together with *My Schools and Schoolmasters*, is that early work *Scenes and Legends of the North of Scotland*, which was first published in 1835 and has been reprinted many times. As well as including local spoken history, family stories, and accounts of traditional customs, *Scenes and Legends* is a wonderful gathering together of supernatural spine-chillers, and accounts of wonders and of fairy belief – most of which Miller would have heard when he was a child, and much of it from his mother who relished these old tales. The enchantment that must have transfixed the young Hugh as he listened to the stories of Stine Bheag the Wind Witch, and Willie Millar's adventures in the Dropping Cave, suffuses the often Gothic atmosphere of his own expansively descriptive retellings. Remarkable for its time, *Scenes and Legends* is more than a general collection of folklore (though this term had not yet been coined), for the stories it contains mostly cluster around one location, Cromarty itself. Because the original tellers would all have been born in the eighteenth century, the book is a unique record of the tales that provided family and community entertainment in a thriving Highland port well over 200 years ago.

Though Cromarty hasn't remained unaltered since the early nineteenth century – apart from anything else, it has grown in size – it is close enough to the town that Hugh Miller knew, for us to be able to wander among the cottages of the old fishertown, to explore the vennels and the graveyards, and to retell some of the stories that he heard when he was a boy.

Let's start at the top of the Paye, the cobbled way that begins above the west end of the town. In the fifteenth century this was part of a pilgrims' route, leading to a ferry across to Nigg and then on to the shrine of St Duthac in Tain (today a four-car ferry still operates between Cromarty and the Nigg peninsula). Now the modern main road sweeps past, bearing down the hill into High Street, past the playing fields and the Victoria Hall. Looking west over the town from the top of the Paye, you can see the Moray coast in the distance, framed by the two opposing cliffs, known as the Sutors, which guard the entrance to the Cromarty Firth. The Sutors – good Scots word – were two giant shoemakers who sat, one on each cliff top, hammering and stitching away. They had only one set of gear between them, so they would toss the tools of their trade to and fro across the water as they cobbled together their seven league boots.

To the immediate left is the Gaelic Chapel. It was built in 1784 by William Ross, a merchant who had grown rich from the hemp trade, to accommodate an influx of Gaelic speakers from the surrounding villages into the largely anglophone Cromarty. Now the chapel is a poor ruin, open to the sky, and inside its shell a wild secret garden has established itself.

Opposite the Gaelic Chapel is a hedgerow, and beyond that to the south are fields. Hugh Miller tells the story of Thomas Hogg, a fisherman, who was returning home to Cromarty on a still, silent night around the turn of the nineteenth century. The light of the full moon was diffused by cloud, but it was bright enough to see pretty well, and Hogg was in good spirits as he walked along the road approaching the town, on the last leg of his journey. The tranquillity was broken by what sounded like the baying of dogs beyond the hedge, close by in the fields, and the startled fisherman imagined that there must be a pack of hounds out hunting there. What might their quarry be at that time of night? He had not the slightest idea. In his pocket he found some crumbs of sea biscuit left over from his last voyage. He held them in his outstretched hand, hoping to calm the animals, but, when he squinted into the field, he saw not dogs but the silhouette of a man. The baying stopped abruptly. 'Well,' said Thomas Hogg, 'that must be the owner put a stop to their racket. I'm safe enough now.'

He kept walking, a little more briskly than before, and saw through the hedge that the figure was keeping pace with him. When they reached a big gap in the hedge, the man in the field turned and began to walk directly towards the fisherman. As the man got closer, his body grew taller and taller, and then he dropped down on all fours and took on the shape of a horse. The ugly, shaggy, limping thing kept pace with Hogg, hurrying on when he hurried, stopping when he stopped, as if it were mimicking him. When the two travelling companions reached the top of the Paye, and the gates of the Gaelic Chapel graveyard, there was a flash like a bolt of lightning, and when Hogg the fisherman's sight cleared, the man-horse had evaporated.

## ~ The Postie and the Ghost ~

By the end of the eighteenth century, a network of mail coaches had been established in Britain, though the service didn't reach Inverness until 1813. In more remote rural areas, including the Highlands, the mail would be delivered by hand, often in relays. The postie was a great carrier of news and gossip, as well as letters and parcels, sometimes staying overnight in a community and ceilidhing there. A little over 200 years ago, the final link in the chain of postmen who brought the mail back and forth the 9 miles from Fortrose to Cromarty was an elderly man whose name was Saunders Munro. One evening, on his way back home, he heard voices raised in argument behind him on the road. Two men overtook him, and he recognised them; one was a tacksman from Cromarty parish, the other a miller from Resolis on the far side of the Black Isle peninsula, dressed, as he always was on high days and holidays, in scarlet hose and tartan, with a big brass pin fastening his kilt at the waist. There had been a fair in Rosemarkie that day and the two were reeling a little from drink as they sniped and sneered over some disagreeable bargain that had been struck earlier.

Munro the postie tried to calm the men down, but they wouldn't be appeased. They reached the Fairy Burn at Rosemarkie and paused, as if they were deciding what their respective ways home would be. There was no sense in the tacksman going along with the miller up the White-Bog Road and over Mulbuie Moor, and Saunders pointed this out to him. His advice only aggravated the situation.

'You think,' said the tacksman, 'because he's bigger than me that I couldn't stand up to him in a fight. Well I'm going with him over the moor, even if it is the long way, just to prove I can take care of myself.'

Saunders Munro tried one last time to separate the pair, but they went off together and faded into the gloom, leaving Saunders with a feeling of impending doom that accompanied him all the way back to Cromarty. Less than two hours after he and the postie parted, the tacksman arrived home, but two days passed and there was no news from the miller. The miller's two sisters asked around, and made some sense of the events that had taken place on the day of the fair. When they called at the tacksman's farm, no one answered their knocking. The door was open so they went in, and found the tacksman alone, staring into the fire.

'We know that you and our brother took the White-Bog Road together,' said one, 'and we hope you can tell us where you parted company.'

The tacksman continued to stare into the fire, shaking his head gently. 'I wish I was able to tell you. I've tried and tried these last two days to recall what happened that night, and it's so hard for me. The thing is, we'd both had more to drink than we should, and I regret that so much. But one thought keeps coming back to me; that we parted company at the Grey Cairn. I think we spent time there, but I can remember nothing after that.'

Though it wasn't far off nightfall, the two girls set off for the Grey Cairn. As they left the farmhouse the tacksman half rose in his seat, perhaps intending to go with them, but then he sat again and fixed his eyes once more on the fire, as if he were hoping that a vision of the events that had taken place that night on the moor would appear in the flames.

Legend has it that the Grey Cairn is the burial place of a Pictish king, killed in an ancient battle whose motives are long forgotten. Light was fading as the girls approached the spot, along one of the many paths that criss-crossed Mulbuie Moor. They felt the cold

wind, and heard its drone as it threaded through the great pile of old stones. Not far off a dog began to howl. As they drew closer they saw that it was their brother's dog, and that it was keeping watch over its master's body.

Next morning, a party of local farmers came to view the miller's corpse. Perhaps the kerchief seemed a little tight, but there were no marks on the neck itself. The body looked as if it had been laid down by a giant hand, for there was no sign of a struggle, or disturbance of any kind, in the surrounding moss and heather. It was a mysterious death, but because there was no evidence of foul play the miller was buried, and no more was said. Herd-boys from the moor built a small pile of stones in the place where the body had been found. It remained undisturbed for many years thereafter.

A couple of weeks after the miller's funeral, Munro the postie was returning to Cromarty through Navity woods at dusk when, for some reason, he glanced over his shoulder and saw a tall figure striding up behind him. He took it to be one of his friends, a local farmer, and stopped, reaching in his pocket for the snuff box so he would be ready to offer a pinch. As the figure got closer, Munro's eye was caught by the glint of a large brass pin. As it got closer still, he saw clearly the red hose and the tartan. He dragged himself away from the place, and stumbled along the path to home, glancing back from time to time to see that the figure was keeping pace with him. Then, at the gate of the Gaelic Chapel burial ground, his pursuer disappeared.

The following evening, as Saunders Munro was coming through Navity woods, the spectral companion appeared again, and again vanished at the gate of the burial ground. The postman determined to leave Fortrose the next day in good time to arrive home when there was still some light. On his return, there was no sign of the ghost in the woods. With a growing feeling of relief Saunders reached the outskirts of the town. The sun was setting as he crossed the street to the haven of his cottage. There, in the dying light of day, the miller's ghost rose up beside him, with a clear expression of silent pleading on its face, and shimmered away as Munro entered the door of his home.

About halfway along the Paye, before you drop down into Cromarty, there's a set of rough-hewn stone steps to your right. Climb the steps, follow a narrow path above the back of the town, and you come to the grounds of Cromarty House, and to woodland which, in Hugh Miller's time, was known as the Ladies' Walk. After three encounters with the miller on three consecutive days, Munro's nerves were stripped to the bare wire. He decided to take a different route back home from his usual one, and to return instead through the woods along the Ladies' Walk. The path crosses a burn which runs along the bottom of a shallow ravine. As Saunders Munro climbed up the bank and out of the hollow, the spectre of the miller appeared at his side, effortlessly keeping pace, gliding through the shrubs and bushes as if it had less substance than an evening mist. When the postman and the ghost reached the ruined wall at the entrance to the old graveyard of St Regulus' Chapel, the miller spoke.

'Saunders, I must talk with you. There's something I need you to do for me.'

Saunders could scarcely speak for terror. 'Whatever you want of me, it won't and can't be possible. Let me be. Please leave me alone.' And he hurried down the Causeway, past the entrance to Thieves Row, and back home. Next day he told his story to the minister, one of the new breed, a clear-thinking, liberal man. He dealt with Saunders like a doctor handing out treatment. So the postie went to see an old farmer who was renowned for being one of 'the Men', a breed of elders whose Christianity was infused more with divine inspiration than puny good sense.

The farmer saw no reason to disbelieve Saunders' story. He arranged to meet him the following evening on Eathie Hill, a few miles to the west of Cromarty, and they would walk back to the town together. Saunders was late returning home that night, and no one ever discovered what passed between him and the farmer, or what happened in Navity woods, but he never saw the miller's ghost again.

The tacksman, too, kept whatever secret he might have had. On one occasion he did accost the farmer who was one of 'the Men'. He was given no audience, just a stern rebuff, and over a short period of time the spirit seemed to drain out of him, leaving him a shuffling, downcast creature and, finally, a corpse on the bier. If he remembered what happened that night at the Grey Cairn, he took the memory with him to the silence of the grave.

# ⁓ The Story of Sandy Wood ⁓

Back along the Causeway, and up a steep, winding hill, is the burial ground of the Chapel of St Regulus, the monk who is said to have brought the bones of St Andrew from Greece to Scotland for safe-keeping. The way in, now a tumbledown path, is opposite the mouth of a dark tunnel which is the tradesmen's entrance to Cromarty House. There is little trace left of the fourteenth-century chapel. The burial ground itself is wild, and shaded with massive yews, and the inscriptions on many of the horizontal grave slabs are full of moss. These, which tend to be the older stones, are inscribed with *memento mori*, including – along with the mattock, the hourglass and the bell – skulls and crossbones. This may be why, today, local children call the place 'the pirates' graveyard'. Sadly, no pirates are buried there, although several of the eighteenth-century seafarers, among them Hugh Miller's buccaneering grandfather, may have been smugglers.

Just outside the burial ground is the grave of Alexander Wood, who died in 1690. His wife and at least some of his children lie at his side. In the past, suicides, witches and unbaptised children have all been denied access to consecrated ground, but Wood was none of these. This is how he came to rest among the outcasts.

Alexander Wood was a man of extreme passions. Although he and his wife were poor folk, no friend who happened to be in their house at a meal time left unfed, and no beggar who knocked at the door was turned away empty-handed. But the most generous man you might hope to meet was also the most malignant harbourer of a grudge. Once crossed, he fermented a hatred inside which was bound eventually to manifest itself in poisonous revenge.

The Woods had a neighbour, a short, stout shoemaker, who was well known in Cromarty for his sly wit and practical jokes. Alexander's intelligence wasn't subtle enough to grasp the wit, but he was sure his neighbour was an honest man because he had an honest face.

The Woods' garden, and the shoemaker's, shared the same piece of ground, which was divided not by a fence, but by four rough

stones. Year by year, Alexander's patch had become less and less productive and, though it couldn't have been possible, his garden actually seemed to be shrinking in size. Finally, he began to wonder whether he was losing his wits. In desperation he started to measure the garden and discovered that it really was getting smaller. How could this be happening? Witchcraft perhaps, or fairy magic? He was completely bamboozled until one spring morning, when he had woken around dawn, he heard a noise in the garden. He went to the window and peered out, and saw the little shoemaker with a crowbar, raising one of the four dividing stones and moving it a couple of inches; not far enough to be immediately noticeable, but still sufficient to increase the size of his own garden by a fraction. Alexander stepped over his window ledge, crept forward and tackled his neighbour round the ankles, and the shoemaker went face down in the soil.

The racket roused the good folk of Cromarty, who came running in their nightcaps and shirts to see Alexander and the shoemaker tussling among the kale and the carrots. The two were parted, which was just as well for the shoemaker, who was coming off by far the worse in the fight. His strength lay in words, not muscle, and he took the opportunity to address the community.

'Friends, forgive me for waking you so early in the morning. I had no choice. The man who I once took to be a good neighbour has been cheating me, and now tries to murder me into the bargain. For a long time I've suspected that my little piece of garden was somehow growing smaller and smaller, but my good nature prevented me from making the obvious judgement. Then for some reason I was awake particularly early this morning. I heard a noise and looked out of the window, and there was this fellow cheerily moving the marker stones in the garden, to the advantage of his own plot. As you know, I'm just a wee fellow, but I was determined not to let him get away with it. I came out and challenged him, and he immediately flew at me with that crowbar. If you hadn't come to my rescue, what doubt is there that I would have been torn to pieces? And look at him. Has he any excuse to offer?'

Alexander was indeed tongue-tied, not with guilt but with rage. The shoemaker's accusations were precisely those he would have made himself, if he'd been allowed to get a word in first. Each time he lunged towards his false neighbour he was held back, and finally he stormed into his own cottage, his rage unvented. It took three days for that rage to subside into a steady, simmering hatred. At first, the fact that he lived next door to the shoemaker gave Alexander some pleasure, for it meant that each time they met, the anger was kindled a little. Eventually, though, he got a mason to build a wall between the two gardens, and it wasn't long after the wall had been built that he realised he was dying.

Alexander was one of the older inhabitants of Cromarty. Among this generation there was a belief that the Last Judgement would be conducted on Navity moor, a few miles to the west of the town. It was his faith in this belief that gave him the strength to call his family to the bedside and tell them that he wished to be buried just a little outside the wall of the chapel, on the Navity side. Being strategically placed there, he would have a head start on the shoemaker when the last trump was sounded. 'Before the wee toad can get his boots on', Alexander would be up on the moor, pleading his case as he'd been prevented from doing when he was alive, and maybe this time he would be heard and believed.

That's the story of how Sandy Wood's grave came to be where it is.

# ⚊ John Reid and the Mermaid ⚊

The hero of the final Cromarty tale is John Reid, who was born at the turn of the eighteenth century. He was an honest, decent man who had built up a career as a shipmaster. He had travelled the seven seas and seen a few of the wonders of the world. Those who dealt with him in business would say that he was solid and reliable, perhaps a little lacking in imagination – not necessarily a bad trait for someone in his line of work.

Now thirty years old, John Reid was just back from a voyage to Holland, and he was wandering round the town in a complete dwam. When folk asked if there was something wrong, he would shake his head mutely, for he was unable to put into words to what degree he was gripped by an emotion he had never experienced before. John Reid was in love. He was in love with Helen Stuart, a delicate but determined creature twelve years his junior. He had first set eyes on her after returning to Cromarty from a long voyage to the Indies, when he was walking along the cliff top of the South Sutor. On the trip to Holland he had been unable to get her out of his mind. Back at home he was kept awake at night by the image of her milky pale face, with its red lips and deep brown eyes peering down at him from the gloom above his bed. When dawn came he would dress, then hover at the threshold, desperate to walk the streets of Cromarty in the hope of meeting her, while at the same time terrified that, if they did meet, Helen might not even glance at him. This fear came close to reality, for when Helen Stuart and John Reid had passed one another that time on the cliff top, Helen had reported to her friends that she had seen a heavily tanned fellow of barely average height, squarely built, whose face, while pleasant enough, seemed to have had its features applied rather too hastily. Helen, like many young women, and many older ones too, had in her head a portrait of ideal manhood, and the mariner bore little resemblance to this portrait.

John Reid returned from Holland in late April. Each day he walked the Cromarty streets, hoping for a glimpse of Helen, but with no success. On May Day, he was out at first light, sure that this time he would be in luck, for this was the day when young girls gathered the morning dew to wash their faces and make themselves beautiful. As the sun rose between the Sutors, he struck out east along the shoreline path to the Dropping Cave. The narrow entrance to the cave has collapsed now, but in the past it was a place for small boys to explore, and the scene of at least one major encounter with the supernatural, when Willie Millar found in its depths a cavern containing a magic horn, and a giant hand which emerged slowly from an ancient tomb. In John Reid's time many strange stories were told about the Dropping Cave, but he gave them no thought. All he wanted was to meet Helen Stuart. As he got closer to the little cove which sheltered the cave, he heard music. It reminded him of an evening in the Hebrides some years before, when he had overheard a woman milking, singing to calm the cow and to make the work go more easily; but the song from the cove was in a language he had never, in all his travels, heard before, and the voice, though captivating, had a chill to it, like the sound of water that has just been released from a frozen burn at the end of a long, hard winter.

John Reid peered out from behind a pinnacle of rock into the cove and saw the figure of a woman sitting on one of the stacks just off-shore. The woman had her back to him, and her long yellow hair spread out over her shoulders and down past her waist. She had a comb in one hand, and a glint from the other suggested that it held a mirror. When a broad fish tail swept round through the water at the base of the stack, John Reid knew that he was looking at a mermaid. Though in all his travels he had never seen a mermaid before, he knew, as all sailors know, the power those creatures have to grant three wishes to anyone who can capture and hold them.

Slowly the mermaid combed her hair, softly she sang. John Reid had the strange notion that deep inside the Dropping Cave a voice was answering her in harmony. He crouched, and crept forward across the thin strip of beach, then sprang over the water towards the stack. He locked his arms around the mermaid's waist. She threw up the mirror and comb, and whistled in anger and alarm like a startled blackbird. She tried to wrestle him into the water. Her strength was alarming but he held her tight until she stopped struggling and lay beneath him, looking up at him with icy green eyes. John Reid thought she must be the most beautiful and the most terrifying thing he had ever seen.

'What do you want from me?' said the mermaid.

'Three wishes.'

'Three wishes, then, and let me go back to the sea.'

'Agreed.'

It wasn't hard for John Reid to decide what his three wishes would be. His father had been a sailor drowned, so the first wish was that neither John nor any of his family should be lost in the same way. The second wish, knowing that Helen was used to a comfortable existence, was continued prosperity for John himself. John Reid only ever shared the third wish with the mermaid, though no one who knew him and Helen ever doubted what it was.

'You have your wishes,' said the mermaid. 'Now let me go.'

John Reid raised himself up, and the mermaid slipped out from under him. She turned in the water and, with a twist of her tail, was gone. John jumped back onto the beach and started to climb the path to the top of the cliff, where he found Helen Stuart, sitting with one of her friends on a grassy knoll above the sheer drop known as Lovers' Leap.

'Of all the people!' said the friend. 'Helen was just this minute telling me her dream of a certain man. Perhaps you can help us unpick its meaning. Last night she dreamed that she was up on the slope above the Dropping Cave, gathering dew just as we've been doing this morning. But there was hardly any dew to be had. The grass and the bushes were dry and brown, and she'd only managed to gather a few drops when she heard someone singing down in the cove. She looked over the cliff edge and you were lying asleep on the beach, and sitting beside you was the singer, who was a beautiful lady. Helen was worried that you wouldn't wake and that you would be covered by the tide; then the next moment you were standing beside her, helping her to shake the dew off the bushes into her jug. She looked for the lady and she was away off on the sea, floating on the water like a white seagull. Then there was a tinkling in the jug, and the drops you were shaking down had turned to solid gold! That was Helen's dream, but there's more. As she and I were walking up here this morning to collect the dew, just as the sun was rising, we heard the strangest singing from down in the cove, and Helen said it was just like the singing she heard in her dream. Now what do you make of that?'

John Reid told Helen and her friend of his encounter with the mermaid – every detail except the three wishes – and, as they went down the hill, her arm was linked with his. They married, of course, and became a family, though Hugh Miller adds a sad little coda to his telling of their story:

> Helen, for the last seventy years, has been sleeping under a slab of blue marble within the broken walls of the Chapel of St Regulus; her only daughter, the wife of Sir George Mackenzie of Cromarty, lies in one of the burial-grounds of Inverness, with a shield of I know not how many quarterings over her grave; and it is not yet twenty years since her grandson, the last of the family, died in London, bequeathing to one of his Cromarty relatives several small pieces of property, and a legacy of many thousand pounds.

# SAINTS AND SORCERY

The Nigg peninsula is just a short ferry crossing north from Cromarty, across the mouth of the Cromarty Firth. It is famous for its Pictish cross-slabs and for the discovery in the late twentieth century of the remains of a Pictish monastery at Portmahomack.

A popular view of the Picts is that they were a mysterious people. But early records from other cultures, and more recent archaeological and place-name research, have made them less enigmatic than had previously been supposed. Living in what are sometimes called the Dark Ages, they were a collection of tribes on the fringe of the Celtic diaspora, inhabiting that part of Britain north of the Antonine Wall, and brought together in a fragile unity to oppose common foes – primarily the Romans, the Dalriadic Scots who came in from Ireland in the west, and the Vikings. It was a Roman commentator who, in AD 297, first wrote of 'picti', the painted ones, and it's been suggested that this might have been a nickname given by Roman soldiers to troublesome adversaries who painted or tattooed their bodies. They spoke a Celtic language, more akin to contemporary Welsh than to Scots Gaelic, and their way of life was probably much like that of their cousins in other parts of the Celtic world. Though at times they fought amongst themselves, they were held together loosely by a system which combined local rulers with a supreme, possibly rotating, overlordship.

The strongest evidence for the cultural sophistication of the Picts comes from those carved stones, which they left in many parts of Scotland, including the Northern and Western Isles, but concentrated in the north-east and Moray Firth areas, and in Perthshire and Angus. These startling and often perplexing monuments appear over a period of 300 years, from around the sixth century, and range from unshaped and incised stones to immensely complex and beautiful relief slabs. The latter swarm on one side with real and mythical beasts, elaborate interweaving ornament, and human figures – typically mounted warriors; and on the other they are decorated with Celtic Christian crosses. No one has yet determined the purpose of these stones and the meaning of the bold symbols – the double-disc, the crescent and v-rod, the 'beast', and many others – which are cut into them, so there is indeed a mystery here.

A major reason for the sense of mystery that surrounds the Picts is the fact that they left no written records that have come to light, apart from a list in Latin of the names of their kings. In Ireland and in Wales, early Christian monks wrote down the traditional myths and legends of the communities in which they lived (and in which some of the monks themselves would have been born). Because of these acts of preservation, we now have the relatively modern bringing together of 'national' stories in collections like the Welsh *Mabinogion* and the Irish *Tain*. But we have no similar compilation for Pictland. If a monk did sit down with his Pictish grandfather to record the old tales, some of which may be hinted at in the human and semi-human figures and the strange creatures carved on the stones, the manuscript has been lost, or is still waiting to be discovered.

By the end of the ninth century – as a result of factors which include Viking depredation, the increasing influence of Christianity and, finally, union with the Scots – the Picts had faded as an identifiable cultural group. Surprisingly, though, in spite of the absence of the written word, we do have some records of stories that were known to the Picts. Here is one of them. It takes place not in the Highlands, but in North Africa.

Egypt in the third century was a hard place to be a Christian. Persecution was widespread and harsh, torments were cruel and ingenious. One young man, who had withstood the hot plates and the rack, was taken out into the desert, smeared with honey, and left to be eaten by the insects and the flies. Another was bound with garlands, and placed on a soft feather bed in a beautiful garden. A young woman appeared. She began to kiss and touch him and, though he tried to sustain pure thoughts, he found he was giving into her tempting caresses. In a moment of inspiration he bit off his tongue and spat it in her face, and the subsequent pain was enough to quell his lust.

About this time, a young man called Paul was living in the region of Thebes. He was well educated and from a well-to-do Christian family, and he had a married sister. When he was sixteen, Paul's father and mother both died, and he thought it would be wise to leave the family home and find somewhere more secluded to live until the persecutions died down. But his brother-in-law, although acting as if he were his best friend, was lured by the promise of a reward and determined to turn Paul in to the authorities. Paul got wind of this, said goodbye to his sister, and headed off into the desert. He penetrated deeper and deeper into the wilderness until, one day, he came to a cave entrance at the foot of a mountain. The entrance was blocked by a boulder. Paul put his shoulder to the rock, rolled it aside and stepped into the cave. It was an enclosure open to the sky. In the middle was a palm tree, and at the foot of the tree a spring spurted out of the earth and its waters disappeared again into an underground channel. In this place Paul made his home, drinking the spring water and eating the fruits of the palm. And every day a raven would fly down with half a loaf of bread in its beak to help keep him alive.

In the year 251, not much more than two decades after Paul came into the world, another young man was born into a wealthy Christian family in the same region. His name was Anthony. Like

Paul he had a sister, and their parents died while the siblings were still in their teens. Not long after he was orphaned, Anthony was inspired by the words of Christ to give away his possessions. He sold everything he had and gave the money to the poor, leaving just enough to provide for his sister, whom he placed in a convent. Anthony himself went to live in a small hut, keeping himself busy with his hands, helping people and praying. But Satan came to tempt him with disturbing thoughts, first about his sister's welfare and about his celibacy, then with visions of a beautiful, seductive woman and of a terrifying child. Anthony resisted every temptation, and Satan retired, feigning defeat, but Anthony knew that his torments had only just begun. He barricaded himself inside a tomb in a cemetery. The only contact he had with the outside world was a friend who brought him food every couple of weeks.

Once Anthony was in the tomb, demons came to beat him up. On one occasion the friend who brought him food found him apparently dead, and took Anthony back to his house; but in the middle of the night he revived and begged to be carried back to the tomb. The assaults continued and at last, at the end of his tether, Anthony demanded to know why he was being punished so severely. The roof of the tomb opened and a beam of light shone down. A voice told Anthony that he would be rewarded for his steadfast resistance to every temptation that had been thrown at him.

There were no more demonic attacks. Anthony went further still into the desert, to a ruined fortress on a mountain top, where he lived alone for twenty years. Once every six months a man delivered food to the fortress. Apart from those visits, Anthony was in total isolation.

When the twenty years had passed, Anthony came down from his mountain. People had expected him to be unkempt and feeble, even driven mad by solitude, and they were astonished by how cheerful he was, and in what good health. He set about founding monasteries, not staying long in any one place, for he was a restless soul. Instead he travelled around, tending to all his flock in turn.

Later in his life, Anthony went to live on top of a mountain near the Red Sea, where he subsisted on a diet of bread, dates and a little oil. Sometimes he made forays to places where Christians were being persecuted – Alexandria in particular – visiting people in prison, speaking out against the regime, and making no attempt to conceal who he was. On these occasions he hoped he might be martyred, but his wish wasn't granted, so eventually he would return to his mountain, where young monks looked after him. There he spent his time praying, weaving mats from palm leaves as a form of contemplation, and tending a small vegetable patch to provide for the visitors who came from far away to see him. One monk, whose name was Macarius, was particularly devoted to Anthony, and would screen visitors, so that only the most spiritual gained an audience with the old man, while the merely curious had to be content with a brief appearance and a homily or two.

One evening Anthony was reflecting on his life. Truth to tell, he was rather pleased with himself, particularly of his status as what he imagined must be the longest enduring and most ascetic of the Christian hermits. As he was contemplating his achievements a voice spoke to him, telling him that there was another who had lived the solitary life a good deal longer, and who was still out in the desert. Furthermore, Anthony should immediately go and find this man, whose name was Paul.

At dawn, taking nothing but his staff, Anthony set off on the quest. He hadn't gone far when his path was barred by a creature which looked like a demonic cross between a man and a horse. Anthony asked if it knew the whereabouts of a brother monk, and the hippocentaur spluttered through its hairy lips in an unearthly language. Anthony made the sign of the cross, and the creature pointed out into the desert before bounding off and disappearing like a mirage. Was it a real denizen of the sands, or the Devil in disguise?

Deeper in the desert, Anthony came to a narrow, rocky valley. A small being with horns, a curled snout, and what looked like goats' feet came out from behind a palm tree. The creature plucked some of the fruit and offered it to Anthony. Anthony asked who, or what, it might be. 'One of the beings mistakenly worshipped as fauns and satyrs,' replied the manikin, 'but in truth we're mortal. And I have been sent to you to plead our case before the blessed Lord who came to save the world.' Anthony was astonished that he could understand what the little thing was saying. He slammed his staff down on the ground, and cursed the pagans of Alexandria who worshipped such monsters, rather than the almighty God. The creature, alarmed by the outburst, spread tiny wings and whirred up into the sky.

At the start of the second day, Anthony found himself on a great desert plain, pock-marked with the tracks of wild animals but with no sight of anything living. He kept going, not having the slightest notion of where he was headed, and as it grew dark he rested close to the lower slopes of a mountain. He heard harsh breathing and looked to see a she-wolf, gasping with thirst, creeping along the foot of the mountain and into the narrow mouth of a cave. Anthony was sure that he had reached his destination. He pulled himself up with his staff and began to shuffle as quietly as he could towards the cave entrance, but he kicked a pebble which clattered and clanged, and, as he looked, a boulder rolled over the mouth of the cave. Anthony threw himself on the ground, berating Paul. 'You let a wild beast in, but you keep me out. I've come so far to find you. I'm not going away. If you don't let me in I'm quite happy to die out here.'

For hours Anthony wailed and pleaded, then from inside the cave came Paul's voice. 'No wonder I don't want to open up, if you've only come here to die!' The stone blocking the cave entrance rolled back. Anthony went in, and he and Paul embraced and kissed. Paul began to question Anthony about the state of the world. Who was in power? Were new houses being built in old places? How was Christianity faring? While they were talking, a raven flew down through the roof of the cave. In its beak was a whole loaf of bread. 'There,' said

Paul, 'all these years and only half a loaf. Someone up there must be watching over us.'

The two holy men then embarked on a debate as to who would break the bread. Anthony said it should be Paul, on account of his seniority. Paul said it should be Anthony, because he was the guest. They wrangled for hours, finally deciding that each would take an end of the bread and pull, and that was how it would be divided.

When they had finished their feast, Paul said, 'Look at me. I'm an old man, with withered limbs and long white hair. Truth is, I'm about to die, and you've been sent to help me on my way to heaven.'

Anthony was distraught. 'After all these years I've only just found you. And now you're abandoning me.'

'Why don't you go and fetch the cloak that Athanasius gave you?' said Paul. 'You can wrap me in it when you bury me.' Paul, who had dressed himself in woven palm leaves for decades, didn't really care either way about being buried in Athanasius' cloak. He simply preferred to die in peace, away from the wailings of Anthony. So Anthony, who had no idea how Paul knew about Athanasius' gift, set off back to his mountain top to fetch the cloak.

Returning through the desert to deliver the cloak, Anthony had a vision of Paul ascending into the heavens, surrounded by clouds of angels. He hurried on, fearing that he would be too late, but when he reached the cave Paul sat apparently praying, hands clasped and face upturned. Anthony sat beside him and prayed too. But after a while he became aware that he couldn't hear the sounds of fervent breathing that accompany prayer. Paul was dead. He had lived for 113 years. Anthony wrapped him in Athanasius' cloak and carried the body that was light as a sparrow's into the desert. There was no spade to dig the grave. Anthony thought of the four-day return journey to bring back an implement, and decided it would be better to die there and then.

The desert sands roiled. Two lions, manes flying, came out of the storm. They started to dig, just deep enough for a grave, and then they raced away. Anthony laid Paul in the grave, covered him with sand, and went back to his monastery. He took Paul's palm leaf tunic with him as a keepsake, and always wore it on the feast days of Easter and the Pentecost.

How can we be sure that the Picts knew this story of the first Desert Fathers? On the cross-slab which is now inside Nigg Church is a triangular panel showing two bearded monks, kneeling with books in their hands. Between them is a chalice, towards which dives a bird holding in its beak not just a loaf of bread, but the consecrated host. The story of the Desert Fathers is undoubtedly here in eighth-century Pictland.

## ~ Stine Bheag ~

Belief in witchcraft is a universal human proclivity. A cow that doesn't give milk, milk that won't yield butter, a run of poor catches at the fishing, a series of failed job applications – someone has 'got it in' for us. In old European stories, that someone is usually what we think of as the typical witch, an old, ugly hag, warty and skelly, who lives in an isolated hovel outside the village. Her comeuppance often arrives with the shooting of a large hare, which has been discovered in the byre, late at night, sucking the milk from the cows' teats. The hare limps away into the darkness and, next day, the witch is found in her cottage bearing a leg wound in the same place that the hare was shot. The witch is a shape-changer. In folklore the story is repeated, with variations, again and again, and the Highlands have many variations from many different locations.

Dornoch in Sutherland, not so far across the open sea from the Nigg peninsula, is where the last witch in Scotland was burned. She was Janet Horne, from Loth near Helmsdale, and she had confessed to shoeing her daughter like a horse, and riding her to meet the Devil. This was in 1722, or perhaps as late as 1727. It was a cold day and poor Janet is said to have warmed her hands by the fire before she was consigned to the flames.

Belief in the possibility of witchcraft is still with us today, of course, even in places that consider themselves to be civilised. Alec Williamson, the great Traveller storyteller, tells a story of his grandmothers. When they were young women, and before they became related by marriage, both were out hawking and landed in the home of a woman in the Black Isle. She made some startling predictions about their futures and they asked if she was the woman they had heard of, who could make the dead herring jump out of the cart. She replied that no, she couldn't do that, but her sister could. However, she was able to set two lovers against each other, just by looking at them.

Records of witch trials like those of Janet Horne, and of the Scrabster witches in Caithness, again in the early eighteenth century, document the persecution and cruel punishment of people who, for whatever reason, had become mistrusted outsiders. But there is good historical evidence that the benefits of witchcraft were also sought for purposes that were not at all malevolent. In the days when the people who lived around the coast travelled primarily by sea, and when fishing and maritime trade were vital to the economy, one particular brand of sorcery was widespread. When he visited Stromness, on Orkney Mainland, in 1814, Walter Scott paid a visit to a wind witch:

> We clomb, by steep and dirty lanes, an eminence rising above the town, and commanding a fine view. An old hag lives in a wretched cabin on this height, and subsists by selling winds. Each captain of a merchantman, between jest and earnest, gives the old woman a sixpence, and she boils her kettle to procure a favourable gale.

Stine Bheag (which in Gaelic means 'little Christina') was a wind witch who lived on Tarbat Ness, on the far north-eastern tip of the Nigg peninsula. Stories are still told about her. How, for instance, because she was a witch, she had been buried outside Tarbat graveyard, but had predicted that she would eventually be inside. The prediction was fulfilled when the churchyard wall was moved to make room for an expanding population of the dead. The following tale of Stine Bheag is my retelling of Hugh Miller's story from *Scenes and Legends of the North of Scotland*.

Each year, in late summer, the fishermen of Cromarty would go north to Tarbat Ness to catch the herring, staying there in makeshift

camps through into the autumn before returning home. In 1738, a band of men under the captaincy of a fellow named Macglashan sailed out of Cromarty harbour, between the north and south headlands which are called the Sutors, and up the coast, past the King's Cave and the Well of Health, past the villages of Shandwick, Balintore and Hilton, past Blacktown and Rockfield, and finally to rest in their customary cove at Tarbat Ness.

The fishing was good. They had the catch salted in barrels when the weather suddenly turned. Incessant rain and a south-easterly wind forced them to shelter under their upturned boat and the canvas sail. The downpour continued, the wind still blew in the wrong direction, and there was no hope of them returning home.

At last, one of the men suggested that they pay a visit to Stine Bheag. Now Stine Bheag was a well-known wind witch. Sailors on the eve of a voyage would go to her to buy a wind that would take them to their planned destination. Macglashan was a stolid man, with little time for superstition, but his crew was insistent. So, the fishermen of Cromarty gathered together what few coins they had and set off through the wind and rain to the other side of the promontory.

Stine Bheag's cottage was the only occupied dwelling in a squat, tumbledown row. Her neighbours had departed long before. They had been unnerved for many years by her strange habits, but the final straw came when her husband and son, realising that she practised the black arts, had determined to denounce her before the Tain Presbytery. Before they could do this, their boat foundered in quicksand, and both of them were sucked down into eternal silence. This had been the neighbours' cue to leave.

Macglashan and his sodden companions came to the cottage door, and the captain knocked. From inside came strange popping sounds, then the door opened and Stine Bheag peered out, a small woman but with a large head and a nose and chin so hooked that they almost met. 'Mother,' said Macglashan, 'we're here to buy a wind.'

'How much will you pay for this wind?' said Stine Bheag.

Macglashan held out a meagre handful of coins, and Stine Bheag looked down at them contemptuously.

'It's all we have,' said Macglashan. 'We need to get back to Cromarty.'

'Fetch that stoup you keep your water in.' Macglashan sent one of the men back to the boat to fetch the stoup, a big stone jar with a narrow neck, and Stine Bheag left the fishermen out in the storm. As she closed the door they caught glimpses of the gloomy interior of the cottage: a pile of bladderwrack that she used to feed the fire, the source of those mysterious popping sounds; a shelf filled with jars and bottles whose contents were unidentifiable; bunches of herbs hanging from the roof beams; and on those beams, hopping and croaking, two giant ravens.

Eventually the man returned with the stoup. The cottage door opened, as if Stine Bheag had known he was back. She took the stoup, told the fishermen to wait, and once more closed the door; when she opened it again she had the stoup in her hands, and a wad of straw was crammed into its neck.

'Take it,' said Stine Bheag. 'Tomorrow you'll have a fair wind. Don't take this straw out of the stoup until you're safe in Cromarty harbour.'

They thanked the old woman and went back to the upturned boat. They crawled under the sail and tried to sleep. Some time in the night they heard the wind die down, and the drumming of the rain diminish to an occasional drop on the canvas. By dawn they were able to put to sea, with a fair wind behind to take them down the coast and back home to their families and loved ones. As they came through the Sutors, and into Cromarty Bay, one of the men spoke: 'If anybody sees us with that stoup, and the straw jammed into it, they'll know we've been dealing with the old wind witch. We'll be preached against on Sunday. We'll be in disgrace. We're almost home. Let's take the straw out now.'

They all agreed this would be a good idea and, in truth, they were curious to see what Stine Bheag had put in the stoup that had made her magic so effective. The crew stood over Macglashan as he removed the straw from the mouth of the stoup. They squinted into the dark interior of the vessel, but could see nothing. Then one of them shouted, 'Look! Look what's coming!'

Cromarty harbour was entirely obscured by the wind-blown rain of a great squall, which hit them so hard it turned the boat around and drove it back through the Sutors, then north past the King's Cave and other familiar landmarks, finally depositing it back on the beach in the cove at Tarbat Ness. And there, sitting on a rock waiting for them, was Stine Bheag. 'What brought you back so soon?' she asked.

The men were too ashamed to answer, and in any case they realised she knew very well what had brought them back. They begged for another wind. She suggested that they try walking back to Cromarty, but finally relented, and that evening they were back home, much humbled and vowing to be more cautious in their dealings with wind witches in the future.

# THE WILD EAST

The road to Cromarty along the northern edge of the Black Isle passes through Cullicudden. Around the turn of the eighteenth century, the minister there had an agreement with his counterpart, who lived in Kiltearn, on the opposite side of the Cromarty Firth; the two agreed that they would take it in turns to remain awake and in prayer throughout the night. They would show their vigilance by keeping a candle burning in one or other window of their respective manses. By keeping watch like this, they would ward off any evil that might be abroad in the darkness on either side of the water.

A couple of years after this pledge had been made, a Cullicudden man was returning late one night over Mulbuie Moor, when he was joined by a stranger. The stranger was urbane and witty, and entertained his companion with humorous anecdotes about the follies of the Church. The man from the Black Isle found himself, quite against his nature, being rather taken by these stories. They carried on jovially until they reached the border with Cullicudden, when the stranger stopped. 'I can't accompany you any further,' he said, pointing across the Firth to the tiny flicker of candlelight in the window of the Kiltearn manse. 'The Watchman is keeping his lookout.'

The stranger faded away into the darkness, there was the distant sound of hooves on stones, and it was only then that the Cullicudden man realised who his companion on the road had been.

Hugh Miller, who relished supernatural legends, knew this story. It makes a fitting introduction to the following selection of tales, which contain a good share of the demonic, both supernatural and human. The last of these east coast stories takes place in Helmsdale, on the Caithness border, but we begin in Evanton in Easter Ross, in the parish of Kiltearn, the home of the Watchman.

## ～ THE LADY OF BALCONIE ～

Behind the village of Evanton is extensive woodland which once belonged to a large estate. Running through the woodland is a deep and narrow cleft called the Black Rock Gorge. The River Glass runs through it, though so deep down that it is often obscured by the trees and foliage that line the sheer walls of the gorge, and the shadows that they cast. Not so long ago, in less cautious times, children used to cross the gorge along the branches that knitted over the drop.

Some centuries ago, the owner of the estate was a bachelor, a man who greatly enjoyed travelling. Sometimes he was away for months and no one knew exactly where he had gone, though people gossiped that Italy was a favourite destination; the city of Padua in particular. One autumn, word had reached the big house that he was to return from a lengthy excursion, and the servants kept a lookout so they could be lined up and ready to receive him. They were amazed when he helped down from his carriage a beautiful dark-haired woman, whom he introduced as his wife.

The new Lady of Balconie could speak no English, let alone the Gaelic that the servants used, and she became a lone and mysterious figure, often glimpsed from a distance, walking among the trees on the estate, going about some business that was kept secret from the rest of the world. However, there was one servant girl she became attached to. No one knew why she had chosen this particular young woman as a confidante, but the Lady had managed to acquire enough Gaelic to communicate her needs, and the girl would often be taken to far-flung corners of the estate, and then abandoned for an age while her mistress slipped off to meet who knows what or whom.

One autumn evening, as it was getting dark, the Lady and her favoured servant were down near the edge of the gorge. The Lady took the girl by the sleeve and began to drag her towards the edge of the chasm, saying how much she loved the place – but the girl held back, for she thought it gloomy and sinister. A tall man dressed in green walked up to them. As soon as she saw him the Lady loosed her grip.

'Time to join me now,' said the man, and took the Lady's hand. She lifted the big bunch of keys from her belt and threw them down onto a rock. The keys sank into the stone, and their mark can still be seen there today.

'I have to go with him,' she said, and the two of them slipped over the edge of the gorge and out of sight.

The servant girl ran back to the big house and told what had happened. Search parties were quickly convened, and for that night and many nights afterwards the surrounding hills flickered with the light of burning torches as the fruitless hunt for the Lady of Balconie continued.

One morning, the master, who had been one of the most fervent leaders of the search, stayed in his room, and a few days later the servants were loading his bags into the carriage as he prepared to make another of his long journeys, though he wouldn't say where he planned to visit.

Some years passed, and no one spoke or thought much about the Lady of Balconie. An elderly retainer, who worked for a woman who lived close to the estate, was down on the lower reaches of the river. He had caught a couple of salmon for his mistress and had hidden another two behind a bush to take home later. His employer surprised him down on the riverbank, and, knowing he could be a rogue, asked him whether he hadn't poached any fish for himself. He assured her that he would never do such a thing and went back with her to the house, carrying her two fish, and protesting his utmost honesty.

Later, when the old man returned to the river to pick up his salmon, there was no sign of them, except for two silver trails which led upstream along the bank. He was determined that no creature, human or other, was going to deprive him of his supper, so he set off to follow the silver trails, first along the grassy verge, then hopping across the stones at the river's edge, until the sheer walls of the Black Rock Gorge began to rise on either side. In the increasing darkness of the gorge, the old man began to lose heart a little, but he carried on, set on recovering his fish. He turned a sharp bend, something he'd never noticed in all the times he'd walked along the top of the gorge, and came into a broad cavern. In the middle of the cavern was a table, and on the table glittered his two fish, with a loaf of bread between them. Next to the table, guarded on either side by a massive hound, and chained to a rusty seat, was the Lady of Balconie.

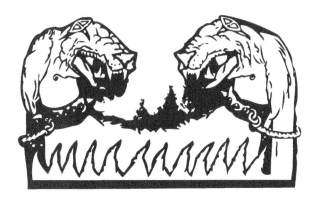

'My dear woman,' said the old man, 'what are you doing here? Where have you been all this time? Come with me and I'll get you back to safety.' For the first time, the giant dogs seemed to notice him. Slowly they turned their heads towards him, and both growled softly.

'I can't go with you,' said the Lady of Balconie. 'He has me prisoner, and he'll be here any moment. Escape while you can.' She took up the loaf, tore it in two and threw a piece to each of the hounds. While they slavered over the bread, the old man turned and left the crepuscular cavern. He stumbled downstream, through the pebbles and boulders of the shallows, and was mightily relieved to get back to his cottage, even without his fish. And that was the last time anyone on earth laid eyes on the Lady of Balconie.

# ⸺ Last Wolves ⸺

A stone in a lay-by on the A9, a few miles south of the Sutherland fishing village of Helmsdale, commemorates the slaying of the last wolf in that part of Sutherland.

It's often said that the very last wolves in Britain roamed the Scottish Highlands until the middle of the eighteenth century, though naturalists think a more plausible date for their final disappearance would be much earlier, perhaps around 1600.

But no one really knows when the last wolf died. We do know that the animals were hunted remorselessly, and that the forests that gave them protection were being continually cut down, so their natural habitat was rapidly vanishing. In earlier times the wolf was seen as a pest, threatening livestock and even human life. Now some of us see it differently, as a beautiful and intelligent creature, threatened by modern civilisation. But in those places where wolves still roam free, farmers will hunt them down and kill them.

Here are three of the many stories about these last lupine survivors and how they met their ends. The first has no particular date, but is still known today in the area of Strathglass, in Inverness-shire. It happened near the well of St Ignatius, which is at the side of the A831, near the village of Cannich.

A woman had gone out just before Christmas to borrow a girdle – a circular iron plate with a handle, used for baking things like scones and pancakes. On her way back home, she sat down on an old cairn to rest and to gossip with a neighbour. There were scrapings and rustling sounds from inside the cairn, and a wolf's muzzle poked out of the stones, just by the woman's side. She lifted up the iron girdle and brought it down on the wolf's head, and that was how the last wolf in Strathglass died. The Inverness storyteller Andrew Mackintosh heard this story from his granny, who came from Strathglass. Alec Williamson, the Edderton storyteller, has essentially the same tale, but in his version the woman stops at the cairn not to gossip, but to perform, as Alec delicately puts it, 'a natural function'.

The second story tells of the very last wolf killed in the Highlands – and so the last in Britain – and is set in Morayshire, just over the Highlands border, in 1743.

A great black beast had killed two children. The Laird of MacIntosh summoned all the best hunters in the area to gather in one place, so that they could join together to track down and kill the creature. When the time came they were all there except for one man, whose name was MacQueen. He was a giant of a fellow, and a famous deer hunter, who lived in a place called Ballachrocin, on the River Findhorn. Eventually MacQueen arrived.

'What kept you?' asked MacIntosh sarcastically.

MacQueen drew the severed head of the 'last wolf' from under his plaid, and tossed it down at MacIntosh's feet. 'I brought him for you,' he said.

The final 'last wolf' tale is the one commemorated on that stone in the lay-by on the A9, just south of Helmsdale. Like the Strathglass story, it is still passed on by word of mouth from generation to generation among the communities in that part of the Highlands. The words on the stone read:

TO MARK THE PLACE NEAR WHICH
(ACCORDING TO SCROPE'S 'ART OF DEERSTALKING')
THE LAST WOLF IN SUTHERLAND
WAS KILLED
BY THE HUNTER POLSON,
IN OR ABOUT THE YEAR 1700,
THIS STONE WAS ERECTED BY
HIS GRACE THE DUKE OF PORTLAND, K.C.,
AD 1924.

William Scrope's *The Art of Deer-Stalking*, which was first published in 1839, was a Victorian bestseller. Its richly yarning accounts of the thrill of the chase are reckoned to have been an important influence on the influx of gentlemen who came in increasing numbers to the hills in pursuit of the elusive stag. Scrope also includes some Highland legends in his book, and this last wolf story is among them.

A matter of yards to the north of the lay-by where the stone is set, there's a sign for Glen Loth, which points to a single-track road forking off steeply from the left-hand side of the A9. If you take this road, in minutes you will be in a glen full of brochs and standing stones, where deer graze high on the mountain slopes.

One morning, a hunter called Polson set off up Glen Loth with his son and another boy. They were tracking a savage wolf which had caused great damage to livestock in the area. Over the brae they went, along by the side of the burn, and past the cairn which was said to be the burial mound of Bran, the favourite dog of the legendary Irish warrior Finn MacCool. When they came to a place where two burns met, they turned west, along Glen Sletdale, and kept going for a couple of miles. As they passed a fall of rocks, they heard whimpering sounds from deep underground. Polson put down his gun, and tried to squeeze through a gap in the rocks, but he was too big a man. He sent the boys through the opening, and they scrambled down into an underground cave. When their eyes got used to the dim light they saw broken eggshells, feathers and bird bones scattered across the floor; and, in the corner, a litter of wolf cubs. The boys shouted up to Polson to ask what they should do, and his answer was to kill the cubs. Just as they took out their knives to begin the slaughter, the she-wolf – the cubs' mother – returned to the den. Before Polson could stop her, she had slipped past his legs and was halfway into the entrance. Polson grabbed her tail, to stop her going any further. Down in the cave, his son shouted up to ask why it had gone dark. 'If this tail comes off at the root,' Polson shouted back, 'you'll know why it's gone dark.' Polson tried to reach his gun, but it was too far away. So he pulled out his hunting knife and stabbed the wolf in the hindquarters, until she was weak enough for him to pull her out of the cave entrance and finish her off.

And that was how the last wolf in that part of Sutherland met her end.

## ~ The Harbour Witch ~

The final two east coast stories here are both rooted in Helmsdale, in the very far north of this part of Sutherland, though the second ranges far afield, from Norway down to Atholl.

Though it has a long history, Helmsdale, as it is today, was laid out as a fishing port in the early nineteenth century, to accommodate people who had been evicted from the inland straths during the Highland Clearances. Fishermen were brought in from the north-east, across the Moray Firth, to teach the dispossessed crofters new skills, and the village thrived in the days when the herring fishing was good.

Back in the late nineteenth century, there were around 150 boats in the area. The fishermen were very superstitious, as fishermen always have been. For instance, if they crossed the path of a minister on the way to their boat, they would go back home. Rabbits were not allowed on board ship, nor were pigs. Quite recently, one Helmsdale fisherman's wife was blamed for a bad day's catch because, for a piece, she gave her husband a pork pie with the image of a pig on the wrapper. And some women in the village were believed to be witches; if the fishermen saw them on their way to the harbour, they would abandon the fishing for the day.

One summer's evening, around the year 1895, the Helmsdale fleet set sail for the fishing grounds. Every boat made a good catch – except one. The skipper of that boat, who was very superstitious, decided that he had been 'witched'.

The next evening, when the fleet set sail again, the fishermen hadn't got far when they noticed a column of black smoke ahead of them. They thought a boat had caught fire, but, when they got closer, they saw it was a replica of the 'witch', floating on the water. She wore a straw hat, and carried a broom in her hand. The model had been made by the man who was convinced he was under a spell. The previous evening, when he was on deck, he'd seen the woman wearing a straw hat, and walking across the sea, from buoy to buoy, sweeping away the fish with a besom. When he told his crew, none of them believed him, so the next day he made an effigy of the woman, complete with broom and hat. In the evening he'd gone ahead of the other boats, set fire to the effigy and thrown it into the water.

When the other boats returned the next morning with a good catch, the effigy was still smouldering. The boat of the man who had 'burnt the witch' was the last in. It was loaded with herring, and he even had to leave some nets in the sea.

Down at the harbour, everyone was talking about the witch when two young men arrived with the news that the effigy had been seen on the shore about a mile from the harbour. It was standing upright with arms outstretched – one of them holding the besom – and quite untouched by fire. The straw hat had gone from its head, and in its place was a tam-o'-shanter. When some of the folk from the harbour went to investigate, there was no sign of the witch. A little while later, a railway surface-man said he had seen a woman on the beach. She had vanished, going either up or down, and leaving no trace behind.

# ⏤ Frakkok's Tale ⏤

Helmsdale takes its name from Old Norse – it means the Dale of the Helmet – and this is a Viking story. It tells of a local woman called Frakkok Moddan's-Daughter, wife of Ljot the Renegade, mother of Steinvor the Stout, and grandmother of Olvir Brawl. She was ambitious, and a smooth operator. The tale is from Orkneyinga Saga, first set down in Iceland around the year 1200; we have no name for the author.

In the twelfth century, Orkney was ruled over by earls, powerful men with strong connections to Norway, as well as to mainland Scotland. It was a time of strong allegiances, shifting alliances and murderous betrayals. Frakkok's story reflects this turbulent society, with complexities of familial relationships, and double dealings, worthy of *The Godfather*. The names of the protagonists alone make the story worth telling. Hold on to your helmets!

Earl Hakon, who had been responsible for the death on Egilsay of his co-ruler Magnus Erlendsson – St Magnus of Orkney – had two sons by his mistress, Helga Moddan's-Daughter. Helga was Frakkok's sister. The sons were Harald Smooth-Tongue and Paul the Silent. When Hakon died, the brothers ruled jointly over Orkney. They didn't get on.

Harald and Paul fell out so badly that they divided the earldom in half. After this, Paul remained on Orkney, while Harald spent much of his time in Caithness, where he held the fiefdom from King David of Scotland.

After Harald and Sigurd the Fake-Deacon had murdered Thorkel the Fosterer, who had been a supporter of Earl Paul, the brothers' followers made them agree to try and bury the battle-axe, and to spend holidays in each other's company. So they came together for a Christmas feast on Harald's estate in Orphir, on Mainland, the largest island in the Orkney archipelago. Helga, their mother, and their aunt Frakkok were both there to take part in the celebrations.

One morning, the two women were sitting quietly in a room, doing needlework, when Harald came in. He'd just got up, and was wearing only trousers and a shift. He saw a beautiful snow-white shirt, stitched with gold thread, lying between Helga and Frakkok. 'Who is the shirt for?' he asked.

'Your brother, Paul,' they told him.

Harald wanted to know what Paul had done to deserve such a fine thing. He took off his shift and began to put on the shirt. The women clutched at him and tried to stop him, but he pushed them away. They wailed and tore their hair, but it was too late. The shirt was on Harald's back. His flesh began to quiver, and he died in agony in front of his mother and his aunt.

Paul the Silent took over the whole of the earldom. He realised that the poisoned shirt had been intended for him, and banished the two sisters, who went first to Caithness, then down to Frakkok's estate near Helmsdale. There Frakkok reared a number of children, including her grandson, Olvir Brawl.

Paul was a good, modest leader. But time passed, political wheels turned, and King Sigurd of Norway granted half of the Orkney earldom to Ronald Kali Kolsson, nephew of Magnus the Martyr. Paul couldn't agree to this, so Ronald sent envoys to Sutherland, to ask Frakkok for support in overthrowing Paul.

This was a shrewd move. Frakkok was now well-connected, through her daughter's marriage, to the Scottish king, and agreed to ally herself with Ronald, and to lead an army against Earl Paul with her grandson Olvir Brawl.

The following summer Ronald got as far as Yell in Shetland, but was sent packing back to Norway by Earl Paul. Around this time Olvir Brawl, with some of his pals, looted a house in Duncansby in Caithness, and burned to death its inhabitants, among them Olaf, who was a supporter of Earl Paul, and father of a man called Svein Asleifarson.

Not long after this, Svein himself got into trouble on Orkney. He was outlawed by Earl Paul, and had to flee to Tiree, in the Hebrides.

In the meantime, Ronald determined to have another shot at establishing himself as Earl of Orkney. He sailed from Norway to Shetland, where he was fondly remembered and got a great reception, and then on to Westray, in the far north of Orkney. Ronald's father, Kol, had wisely advised him to promise to build a minster in memory of his uncle Magnus (St Magnus' Cathedral in Kirkwall) if the Orkney folk would support his bid for the earldom. This paid off, and his following on the islands grew.

Svein Asleifarson, back in the picture and now a supporter of Ronald, sailed up to Orkney. He kidnapped Earl Paul while he was on an otter hunt, and spirited him away down to Atholl in Scotland, where Paul's sister, Margaret, was married to Earl Maddad. Paul was in a sticky situation. He offered to leave Orkney forever and go into a monastery, suggesting that Svein spread the rumour that he'd been blinded or mutilated. If this story leaked out, he said, his followers wouldn't come after him.

No one knows what finally happened to Paul, but it was rumoured that his sister Margaret paid Svein to have him 'disappeared'.

Svein was still seeking revenge for his father Olaf's death at the hands of Olvir Brawl. He asked Ronald for help. Ronald tried to dissuade him from going against Olvir and his grandmother Frakkok, who was now an old woman, but in the end he gave Svein two fully-equipped ships.

Svein travelled by Moray to Atholl, and then made his way back up to Sutherland through the hills and mountains, keeping clear of the settlements. Though Frakkok and Olvir had been warned of an impending attack, they expected it to come from Orkney, and had lookouts posted facing in that direction. But Svein came from behind the farmhouse, and took them by surprise. Olvir came out with his men to meet Svein, but they were soon driven back. There was terrible slaughter.

Olvir managed to escape up the River Helmsdale and over the mountains to the Hebrides, where he vanished from history. Svein and his men looted the farmhouse and burnt everyone inside. Frakkok died in the flames, and that was the end of her.

And that is the story of the poisoned shirt.

# HIDDEN KINGDOMS, MAGIC LANDS

The final group of stories ranges across the northern coastline, from the eastern tip of the Caithness flatlands, to Cape Wrath in the far west of Sutherland.

This is a region of particular physical beauty, running through moorland and mountain, across the Kyle of Tongue and around Loch Eriboll, past shortbread-coloured beaches and hidden selkies' coves; but it's also a place where savage battles have been fought, and a place once notorious for witchcraft and magic, whose communities still remember the injustices that were suffered during the nineteenth century Highland Clearances.

The people of Caithness, the location of the first story, are adamant that their county is a place apart from the Highlands, sharing a Scandinavian heritage with Orkney and Shetland, and there is a great dispute as to whether Gaelic was ever spoken in the most easterly parts.

## ~ The Seal Killer ~

Duncansby Head is a little to the north of John O'Groats. Some years ago, I walked from the lighthouse there, down towards the stacks that protrude from the seabed like giant prehistoric arrowheads. In the bay, the black heads of a dozen or so seals rose and turned to look up at me, reminding me of the many stories which tell of the people of the sea.

In a cottage on Duncansby Head, there was once a man who made his living from killing seals. When he had killed them he would strip off the skins to make trousers and waistcoats, boots that were called rivlins, and small purses for ladies to keep their money in.

Six days a week, he would climb down the steep path to the beach, push out his boat, row into the middle of the bay, and wait for the seals to come to him. With him he took a little silver whistle which he had from his father, who had it from his father before him; and so on, back through the generations. With the whistle came a tune, a seal-calling tune. When he played, the seals would gather round the boat to listen.

One day the seal killer was out in the bay, playing his silver whistle, when a huge seal broke the surface of the sea, just by the boat. The seal killer put down the whistle and picked up his bone-handled knife. He plunged it deep into the back of the seal, just behind the head, but the seal was so large and powerful that it dived down beneath the waves, taking the knife with it.

The seal killer was astonished and dismayed. The knife had been passed down to him with the whistle. It was old, and knew how to do its job. He used it to kill the seals, and to skin them, and without it he couldn't carry on with his trade. He rowed back to the shore, climbed up the path, and entered his cottage. He sat down at the kitchen table with his head in his hands, and wondered how he could ever get another knife.

All day the seal killer sat. Evening brought a storm, thunder and lightning. The seal killer drifted in and out of sleep; then, after midnight, someone knocked. He went to the door and opened it. A tall man stood at the threshold, a stranger, with a black cloak wrapped round him, and a wide-brimmed black hat pulled down over his eyes.

'Are you the seal killer?'

'Yes I am. What do you want with me?'

'I've a job for you. You must come with me now.'

There was a flash of lightning, and the seal killer caught a glimpse of a black stallion standing patiently at the cliff edge. The tall stranger climbed into the saddle and pulled the seal killer up behind him, and they rode off into the mouth of the night. They rode through the deepest, darkest valleys, across raging torrents, over the highest mountain peaks, through rain and hail and sleet and snow, until they came to a high cliff top.

The stranger dismounted. So did the seal killer. The stranger wrapped his arms around the seal killer, and took a deep breath. He put his lips to the seal killer's lips, then he blew the air out into the seal killer's lungs, and threw himself off the cliff with the seal killer still in his arms. The two of them fell like stooping hawks until they hit the surface of the sea, and sank down to the ocean's bed.

When they reached the sea floor there was a door. They went through the door and they were in a hall full of brown-eyed, pale-faced, weeping people. The stranger took the seal killer into a smaller room. In the room, on a bed, lay a beautiful woman. She was so pale and still that it was impossible to tell whether she was alive or whether she was dead. The seal killer saw that the handle of his knife was sticking out of her shoulder. Then the stranger spoke.

'This is our queen – the Queen of the Selkie people. Yesterday morning you stabbed her in the back, and now you are the only one who can save her. You must pull out the knife and kiss the wound.'

What could the seal killer do but obey? He leaned forward, pulled out the knife and kissed the wound, and the wound closed over as if by magic. The woman opened her eyes and looked into the eyes of the seal killer, but before either of them had time to speak the stranger said, 'Right, that's your job finished. Come with me.'

He took the seal killer by the arm and led him back through the room full of brown-eyed, weeping people, 'til they came to the sea door.

'Now,' said the stranger, 'before I let you go, promise me one thing.'

'What's that?'

'You will never, ever kill another seal.'

'No, I never will kill another seal.'

'Right,' said the stranger, 'take this, and whatever you do, don't open it until you get home.'

The stranger reached under his cloak and pulled out a bundle. He pressed the bundle into the seal killer's hands, opened the sea door, and pushed him out into the darkness. The seal killer rose and rose through the dark waters until he thought the lungs would burst out of his body. Then his head broke the surface of the sea.

It was dawn, and he was in the bay below the cliff where his cottage stood. He swam to the shore and dragged himself dripping up the cliff path. He opened the door of the cottage and threw the bundle down onto the kitchen table. The bundle split open, and the kitchen was filled with gold coins.

The seal killer never did kill another seal. He lived out his life in the little cottage above the bay. He never married and he never had children. But the people who live in that part of the world say that, whenever the moon was full, he went down to the beach and stood at the edge of the sea. Then he took out a silver whistle, and played a tune. After a while, a great seal pulled itself up out of the sea, onto the shingle. Then the seal took off its skin, and out stepped a beautiful woman. All night long, she and the seal killer danced together on the beach. Then, when the sun rose, the Queen of the Selkies slipped back into her skin, and flopped away into the waves.

# ⁓ How the Sea Became Salt ⁓

The Vikings knew Scotland well, and Caithness in particular. As the story of Frakkok tells, in the early Middle Ages, when Orkney and Shetland were under Norwegian rule, the mainland was used strategically by feuding factions. But Scandinavian settlers also came to farm, as they did in other places throughout northern Britain. Place names like Wick, Thurso, Durness, Melness, Helmsdale, Cadboll, and many others around the north and east coasts and elsewhere, derive from Old Norse, and are evidence of the Norse presence.

The Vikings were great lovers of stories, and the settlers brought their tales with them. One in particular has taken root. It was first recorded by the Icelander Snorri Sturluson, in the early thirteenth century in his *Prose Edda*.

A very long time ago, the King of Denmark was called Frodi. When Frodi ruled, there was no crime – no muggings, no robberies, no vandalism, no murders, no street riots. So those times became known as 'Frodi's Peace'.

In Frodi's palace there was a room, and in that room was a huge mill, which was called the Grotti Stone. It was like the most ancient mills, which are sometimes called querns, where one circular stone is turned on top of another; grain is put into a hole in the middle of the uppermost stone, and emerges from a side channel as flour. But the Grotti Stone was a magic stone. When turned it could grind out anything you asked for, your heart's desire. Frodi's dilemma was that no one in Denmark was strong enough to move it, even an inch, so it lay idle in that room in his castle.

Then, on a visit to his friend the Queen of Sweden, Frodi clapped eyes on two of the palace slaves. They were huge girls, sisters, and their names were Fenya and Menya. Frodi thought to himself – these girls look big and strong enough to turn the Grotti Stone. So he bought them from the Queen of Sweden, and took them back home to Denmark. He had them brought to the room in his castle where the Grotti Stone lay.

'There you are, girls. See what you can do.'

Fenya took the big wooden handle on one side of the stone, Menya the handle on the opposite side, and they began to push. The Grotti Stone ground into motion.

Frodi stared. Slowly he rubbed his hands together. 'Grind me gold,' he whispered.

Gold began to trickle, and then pour out of the great mill. Soon the room was full of gold, then the palace, and it wasn't long before Frodi had to put up sheds to house it. Day after day, week after week, Fenya and Menya turned the stone. After a couple of months, they asked Frodi if they could rest, just for a while. 'No!' said Frodi. 'Keep turning.'

Not long after, they asked again. 'You can stop turning for as long as it takes the cuckoo to sing his song,' was Frodi's reply.

Fenya and Menya took this to be a refusal, since the cuckoo's song is only two notes long. They kept grinding, for after all they were slaves, and had to do as they were told. But in the middle of the night they began to sing a song:

> Frodi is a wicked king – grind, grind the Grotti Stone
> We don't want to grind his gold – grind, grind the Grotti Stone
> Grind an army against Frodi…

And that's what they did. They ground out an army, and the army was led by a king called Mysing. Mysing and his skeleton crew arrived in longships some time after midnight, on the beach below the cliff on top of which Frodi's castle stood. They crossed the shingle, quiet as cats, and scaled the cliff as if their bodies had no weight at all; and they stood facing the castle.

There were no guards, no army. There was no need for such protection, because this was Frodi's Peace, so Mysing and his men mounted the palace steps unhindered. They threw open the oak doors and entered the marble hall. Then they climbed the stairs and went along the upper corridor to the very last room. With a feather's touch Mysing opened the door, and there was King Frodi sleeping peacefully on a bed of solid gold. Mysing slipped his axe from his belt, and crossed the room to the side of the bed. He lifted the axe high and brought it down hard, and in one blow Frodi's head was severed from his body.

Mysing took Fenya and Menya and the Grotti Stone on board his ship, and set sail in a south-westerly direction, heading towards

Scotland. When they were out in the open sea, Mysing looked at the stone and at the two giant girls.

'Grind me... salt!' he commanded, for in those days salt was a precious commodity which graced only the tables of the rich. Fenya and Menya started to turn the Grotti Stone, and out came salt. Halfway across the North Sea, the boat was way down in the water under the weight of its freshly ground cargo.

'Mysing, we should stop,' said Fenya and Menya, 'or the boat will sink.'

'No! Keep grinding!'

So Fenya and Menya kept on grinding and the boat grew heavier and heavier until, just as they reached the island of Stroma in the Pentland Firth, it sank to the bottom of the ocean. Today, in the place where Mysing's ship went down, is a whirlpool named the Swelkie. It's a dangerous whirlpool but, if you sail close enough, you can hear, from deep beneath the waves, the singing of two giant girls. On the ocean's bed Fenya and Menya are still grinding. That's the reason there's a whirlpool in the Pentland Firth; the Swelkie is caused by the sea being drawn down into the middle of the Grotti Stone as it turns. And that's also why, if you take a handful of sea water, put it to your lips, and drink, it tastes of... salt.

Essie Stewart was six weeks old when, in 1941, she was adopted by Mary Stewart, the childless daughter of Alexander Stewart, who was known as Ailidh Dall – Blind Sandy. The family were well-known and well-respected Highland Travellers. Their winter base was at Remarstaig, close to the little market town of Lairg in Sutherland. During the winter months, out in the stable, Ailidh Dall would make utensils out of tin – different sizes of jugs, basins and pails, as well as vegetable strainers – and Essie, when she was old enough, would go to school. Come the spring, probably some time in late April, the family of three would take to the road, with a cart, two horses, and two dogs. Even the family cat would go along for the ride. On the cart was everything that was needed for the summer's camping – bedding, crockery, cutlery, pots, pans, clothes – as well as a tent which would be constructed from hazel boughs and covered with tarpaulins, and a stove for heat and cooking to go in the middle of the tent. That wasn't all. There still had to be room for the goods that would be hawked in the country areas: the hardware – 'pins and needles and threads and combs and brushes and that sort of stuff' – from Robert Ogilvie's in Aberdeen; shirts, underwear, overalls and aprons from Telford's in Lancashire; and the net for net curtains, from a firm in Ayrshire.

Once the Stewarts were on the road, depending on the weather, they would either head west by Loch Shin to Laxford Bridge, or north to Altnaharra, a two-day journey from home. From Altnaharra there were two possibilities for travel: north-east along Strathnaver to Bettyhill, then continuing east into Caithness; or north along the side of Loch Loyal to Tongue, then striking out west on a big circuit that took in places like Durness, Kinlochbervie and Scourie.

One of the stops was at Midtown, on the Melness peninsula, on the western side of the Kyle of Tongue. Like that of his daughter and his granddaughter, Ailidh Dall's native language was Gaelic.

He was a celebrated storyteller, who knew many of the old tales. When the Stewarts arrived at Midtown, Essie recalls:

> …before the tents went up, they would gather; and I can visualise … my mother would be sitting out, and there was a lovely family just along the road – there was two girls, probably eighteen, nineteen year old girls – and they would come along with their teacups to my mother, and she would have to read their cups. And then of course at night they would all be at the tent and my grandfather would be telling stories – telling the Ossian story.

Many years later, long after she had stopped travelling, Essie met a man from Melness, who told her that the campsite at Midtown had been named Cùil Oisein – Ossian's Corner – by the local people, in memory of Ailidh Dall:

> My grandfather had that gift that, whatever story he was telling, he told it in such a way that you would actually think that he knew these people personally. He took on that mantle – he lived the character. He made that story come alive, and that to me is such a great gift. He talked about Ossian as if he was his best friend.

The Death of Ossian, son of Finn MacCool, is one of the great pieces in the Gaelic storytelling repertoire. Here is Essie's own translation into English, from her grandfather Ailidh Dall's version.

❖

They were three shielings, three bothans. One stormy night a woman came looking for shelter. She went to the first bothan and she knocked on the door. A man came out, took one look at her, and slammed the door in her face. She went to the second bothan, and the same thing happened. The third door she went to was Ossian's bothy. She knocked on the door and Ossian came out, and he looked at her and he said, 'You'd better come in.'

So, she went in. Stormy, stormy night – the poor woman was soaked to the skin. She sat beside the fire. Ossian had a big fire on. He fed her supper, and come bedtime he said to her, 'Well look,' he said, 'there is only one bed. Where are you going to sleep?'

'Well Ossian,' she said, 'we've shared a table. Why can't we share a bed?'

He said nothing. She was so ugly, he was afraid to open his mouth. Anyway, he went in one side of the bed, she went in the other, but he didn't sleep. And some time later – early hours of the morning – he put down his hand, picked up his sword, and put the sword between them in bed. Probably exhaustion overtook him, because he dropped off; and when he woke in the morning he looked, and this ugly creature that had gone to bed with him no longer existed. Lying beside him was the most beautiful woman that he had ever seen in his life. He gently picked up the sword, and took it out of the bed, and she turned and she looked at him, and she said, 'You wouldn't have done that last night Ossian.'

'Well no,' he said, 'I wouldn't. Could you blame me?' He said, 'The kind of state that you came in last night, could you blame me?'

'If you ever mention,' she said, 'the ugly way I looked when I came to you last night, I will not spend another hour with you. I will have to leave.'

Anyway, she was there, and Ossian married her. He was doing what he normally did – he was away on the hill, and he was hunting and he was fishing. Ossian was famed for his dogs, and one day he said to her, 'Now look,' he said, 'there's a bitch out there that's due to have puppies. I'm going away, and I won't be back 'til this evening. When the first puppy is born, I want you to put a red ribbon around its neck, and whoever comes to the door – it doesn't matter who it is – if they ask for the puppy, you are not to give that pup away.'

'Very well,' she said. So the morning wore on and she was back and forth to where the dog was, and keeping an eye on it, and eventually the first pup was born. So she went away and got a red ribbon, and tied it on the puppy's neck.

Later on that day, this man came knocking on the door, and he said to her, 'Is Ossian in?'

'No,' she said, 'Ossian is not in.'

'Has the bitch had her puppies yet?'

'Yes,' she said.

'Well,' he said, 'I want the first pup.'

'Oh no, no,' she said, 'you cannot have the first pup. The last thing that Ossian said to me this morning, when he went away, was that whoever came to the door I was not to give the first puppy away.'

And he caught her by the throat and he said, 'I want the first puppy.'

Poor woman, she was so frightened, she went away and she got the pup, and she handed the puppy to him, and took the ribbon off its neck and put the ribbon on one of the other puppies that, by this time, had been born.

That evening Ossian came home in a hurry, and the first thing he said to his wife was, 'Has the bitch had the puppies?'

'Yes,' she said.

'And,' he said, 'did you put a ribbon on the firstborn?'

'Yes,' she said.

So out he went, and picked up the pup by the ear and shook it, and came back in and said to her, 'That's not the firstborn.'

She said, 'That is.'

He said, 'That is not the firstborn.' And an argument broke out, and whatever Ossian said to her, in Gaelic we say, '*Oho! A'bhana-bhuidseach* – you ugly old witch!'

As soon as he said it, she went off up the chimney as a black raven. And Ossian followed her, for how long, or for what distance God only knows.

He was away for years.

And eventually she took pity on him. She came down out of the skies, and she said to Ossian, 'Go back, for God's sake, go back. Because I will never come back to you,' she said. 'Ever.'

She put a gold ring in his hand. She said, 'You put that ring on your finger, Ossian, and you will have health. Now,' she said, 'turn, and go home.' And off she went.

So Ossian turned, and he came back, and it took him a long, long time to come back to his own place; so long that he didn't recognise when he came to the shielings. He didn't recognise any of it. And the first bothy he went into, he opened the door, and sitting at the fireside was Para Naomh-Clèireach – St Patrick. And St Patrick looked at him, and he said, '*Thàinig thu air ais, Oisein* – you've come back Ossian.'

'Oh yes,' he said, 'I've come back.'

This young lad came in, and he had a deer on his shoulder. He put the deer on the table, and St Patrick turned to Ossian and he said, 'Have you ever taken a deer of that size out of your hills?'

Ossian looked at him, and he said, 'I have seen the leg of a black-bird bigger than the deer that you've got on your table.' St Patrick didn't believe him. Ossian was furious, and in the morning he said to this young lad, 'Right,' he said, 'call the dogs. We're going hunting.'

And off they went. They walked for miles and miles, and eventually he said to this boy, 'Bend your head down,' and the boy bent his head down. He put a steel band on his head. 'Now,' he said to the boy, 'lift your head.'

The boy said, 'I can't.'

'Lift your head,' he said to the boy.

The boy said, 'I can't. My head is like to split.'

'*O, Dhia, beannaich mi*,' he says, 'lift your head for goodness' sake.' Eventually he lifted his head, and Ossian let out one roar.

He said to the boy, 'What can you see?'

And this boy says, 'I can see deer such as I have never seen before.'

'Och,' Ossian said, 'let them past,' and he did the same thing the second time. 'Put your head down, he said to the boy, and he put the steel band on his head. And if the first roar that Ossian gave was loud, the second one was even louder. The poor boy, he could barely lift his head, but eventually he did.

'Now,' Ossian said, 'what can you see?'

'Well, well,' he says, 'if the first lot of deer were big, this ones is even bigger.'

He says, 'Let them past.'

The third time he put the steel band on his head, and Ossian roared so loud the rocks split. 'Now,' he says to the boy, 'lift your head.'

He said, 'I can't. I can't lift my head.'

'Och,' he said, 'for goodness' sake lift your head – try and lift your head.' The boy lifted his head. Ossian said, 'What can you see now?'

'Well,' he said, 'if the first lot of deer and the second lot of deer were big,' he said, 'this is the biggest yet; and there's one in particular.'

'Right,' he said. 'Now,' he said to the boy, 'up there in front of you, what can you see?'

The boy said, 'It's like a tree, but I don't know if it is a tree.'

'That's fine,' Ossian said, 'make on it, make to that tree, and when you get to it, climb up. And when you reach the top,' he said, 'let your weight back, and tell me what you can see.'

The boy went to this tree or whatever it was, and he climbed, and he looked; and he saw dogs. There was one dog in particular – a yellow dog – and Ossian said, 'What can you see?'

'Well,' he said, 'I'm seeing dogs, a lot of dogs. But,' he said, 'there's one in particular, she's different to the rest of them, she's a different colour.

'Ah, *Biorach a'Bhuidheag*,' Ossian said, and he whistled, and the dog came. 'Now,' he said, 'we're going hunting.' And Ossian let the dog go, and she went after the big deer, the big stag. Herself and the stag fought it out, and eventually she put the stag on the brink of his back.

Ossian said to the boy, 'Now,' he says, 'what you have to do now – obviously you have to gralloch it and skin it, and then,' he said, 'you will build a fire, and you will boil it – boil that stag.'

The young lad did as he was told, and eventually he cooked the meat. He was handing it to Ossian, and as he was handing it to Ossian he took an inch of the flesh and put it in his mouth. When it was all gone, Ossian said, 'Did I get all of that stag?'

'Yes,' the boy said.

'Well,' said Ossian, 'yes and no. It didn't do you much good, and it's done me a lot of harm. That inch of flesh you stole has marked my eye.' And it was then, they were saying, that Ossian began to lose his sight.

'Now,' he said to the young lad, 'you must be hungry.' He says, 'Take the bow and arrow, go down to that meadow there,' he says, 'and you will see blackbirds. Get one of that blackbirds,' he said, 'take it back here, and you can roast it for yourself on that fire, but,' he said, 'you'll keep one leg.'

So the lad went down and he caught this huge blackbird; he took it up and plucked the feathers off it, and he roasted whatever he wanted to eat and kept one leg.

'Now,' said Ossian, 'let's go home.'

They went back, and Ossian was carrying the leg of the blackbird on his shoulder. He went into St Patrick, and he threw the leg of the blackbird on the table, and the four legs went from under the table. He turned on him and he said, 'Are you calling an old man a liar now?'

St Patrick said, 'Oh well, well, no,' he said, 'I'm not. That is definitely bigger than the stag that was brought in here.'

Ossian was aged, and he had practically lost his sight completely, and one day he said to this young boy, 'Take me down to the loch side, 'he said, 'so that I can have a wash.'

And the boy led him down to the loch side, and when he was washing himself, Ossian took the gold ring that his wife had given him off his finger, and he put it beside him on a stone. And she came swooping out of the sky, the raven, and she picked up the ring and off she went. And Ossian knew that his time had come. So he turned to the young boy and he said, 'Well look,' he said, 'you have seen things that no one else has seen. You have heard things that no one else has heard. But,' he said, 'you will never repeat them.' He caught the young lad, and he broke his neck; and Ossian himself passed away.

Sir Donald Mackay, Chief of the Clan Mackay, who was born in 1590, was created first Lord Reay by Charles I in 1628. An unwavering supporter of the Protestant cause, he led an eventful life in turbulent times. He acquired a reputation for harshness to his tenants, on lands which extended from Cape Wrath to west Caithness, and further afield. His military involvement in the Thirty Years War, though, brought financial strain which meant that he had to sell off portions of his territory. In 1646, after support for Charles was lost, Mackay left Scotland. He died three years later, an exile in Denmark.

After his death, Donald acquired a second, legendary, existence as a wizard. The entrance to this parallel world of spells and sorcery is through a historical portal, for it's said that it was during the Thirty Years War, when he was serving under King Gustavus of Sweden, that Donald first met the Devil. The two got on well, and Satan suggested that Donald might like to attend his Black School in Padua. Donald took up the invitation, and proved to be by far the most talented student in the class; but at the end of his studies he indulged too much in celebrating his academic success. He had forgotten that, on the final day of term, the Devil would always claim the last student out of the classroom for his own. When graduation was over, there was a great rush for the door, and Donald was the only one left in the room. Befuddled though he was, he still had enough presence of mind to utter the now-famous command, 'De'il tak' the hindmost!'

The Devil made a grab for what he took to be the last straggler, but was left clutching only Donald's shadow. Donald made a hasty getaway, and the Devil was so furious that he packed his bags and followed the man who had tricked him back to Scotland, determined to give him back his shadow and claim his soul. They met in Smoo Cave, on the coast in the far north-west of Sutherland, and the two of them started to fight. The brawl lasted for days. A lot of boulders were thrown and bolts of lightning cast, and finally Donald appeared to gain the upper hand. His prize was a small box, which contained an army of imps, desperate to work for whoever the box's owner might be.

After his apparent victory, Donald began to wonder whether the Devil hadn't, after all, taken sly revenge for the deception over the shadow. The little chaps in the box were not just keen to work, they were voracious. Most tasks were completed in a few hours, and nothing seemed to take them more than a couple of days. Then they would be back, nipping and scratching, and demanding, 'Give us a job, give us a job!'

One day, Donald thought of a task which would be to his advantage if it could be accomplished. There were tales that a pot of gold was hidden in a loch near Broubster, south-east of Reay, so he set the imps to draining it (the hills of Creag Mhòr and Creag Bheag remain today as evidence of their skills in excavation). As the work was progressing, the Cailleach of Clash Breac was passing by, and demanded of the imps, 'In God's name, what are you up to?' The tiny labourers couldn't bear to hear the name of the Almighty, and vanished instantly. Donald was furious. He lifted a spade and brought it down on the Cailleach's head, and split it in two, and the boulders that were once the Cailleach's skull can still be seen in that place.

The imps must eventually have returned to their master, because he often took them to Caithness, where they were in great demand for their agricultural accomplishments. At the end of one particularly cold and stormy summer, the farmer at Lythmore had been unable to take in his harvest. Donald showed up at the door one evening, and promised to have the harvest cut, bound and stooked by the end of the following day.

The next morning was sunny and still. The farmer went to Donald, who was still in bed, to tell him that it was a good day for the harvesting. Donald turned over and started to snore loudly, and he stayed in his room until the sun had almost set. Then he sauntered out into the field with a sickle in his hand, cut a swathe of corn, bound it into sheaves and stacked the sheaves. He stood back and said, 'All the same as this one.' A thousand invisible hands set to work, and soon every stalk of corn on the farm was harvested, tied and standing in a stook.

Eventually, Donald grew weary of the pestering of the imps. He set them to building a bridge, made from the sands of Dunnet Bay, across the Pentland Firth. The imps flew into action. Ropes of sand unfurled across the water – but, just as the bridge was about to reach the island of Hoy, the tide changed and it was washed away. Donald left the imps there, and even today they are still trying to build that bridge, never quite managing to get to Hoy before the tide turns.

No one seems to know whether, in the end, the Devil managed to snare Donald Mackay's soul. There may have been some late, death-bed, visitation, but I heard that the last time they met was again in Smoo Cave. The meeting was in a boat, on the underground lochan in the smaller chamber behind the main cavern. Donald had taken his dog with him for protection, but there was little hope for his soul. Some time in the past a terrible deal must have been done, and the Devil held a contract which was only waiting for Donald's final, confirming signature. Then, just as the pen scraped its first mark on the parchment, outside in the cold distance a cockerel crew. The Devil's powers evaporated with the dawn. Donald rowed away to safety, and Satan himself, in his fury, blasted out through the roof of the cave – the hole, one of several, is there today. But the dog… the dog never came out of Smoo Cave. Two weeks later it came out of another cave entirely, some 20 miles down the coast. No one knows where it had been or what it had seen, but when that dog emerged from the darkness there was no hair, and hardly any skin, left on its body.

# — The Highwayman —

Smoo Cave is a huge limestone cavern, the largest coastal cave in Britain. It's a couple of miles to the east of the community of Durness, in the very far north-west of Sutherland. There are signs of occupation going back to Mesolithic times, and the word 'smoo' is derived from Old Norse, signifying a cleft or a creek. Either meaning would be appropriate: the cave is set at the back of a narrow, steep-sided cove; and the Allt Smoo burn enters through a sinkhole in the roof of the secondary cavern as a 25m-high waterfall. The water then gathers in the lochan where Donald Mackay met the Old Lad, and from there flows out of the mouth of the main cave, and down to the sea.

The cave is now illuminated with electric lights, but, not so long ago, in more superstitious times, it would have been a dark and sinister place, and ideal for concealing the murdered victims of highway robbery. This, indeed, is what a character known locally as the Highwayman did with the bodies of eighteen or more souls, tipping them down through the sinkhole into the murky, eel-infested waters of the lochan below.

The Highwayman has been called by various names – MacLeod, MacMurdo, MacMurchey – and his grave slab inside Balnakeil Church is inscribed Donald Makmurchou. Let's call him MacMurchey. A favourite story about this notorious malefactor tells of an incident which happened towards the end of his life.

The daughter of Alexander Munro, the Durness minister, was to be married to the son of Donald Mackay, the first Lord of Reay, and legendary sorcerer. Munro had been visiting his daughter's future father-in-law in Tongue, and Sir Donald had insisted that, on the return journey, the minister be accompanied by an armed man for safety. The minister had heard a rumour that MacMurchey was sick and not long for this world. As he would be passing the Highwayman's cottage on his way back to Durness, he decided to call on him and try to redeem his soul. MacMurchey would have none of it. He sent the minister packing, and would have killed him if the armed man hadn't been there.

The Highwayman had two sons, who had been away from home when the minister called. Their father, still raging at the holy man's impertinence, sent the two lads after him, with orders to murder both him and the bodyguard, and bring back Munro's heart. Their courage failed them. They caught a ewe, killed it, and cut out its heart, instead of the minister's. When they brought it back to their father he examined it contemptuously.

'I always knew the Munros were cowards,' he said, sensing his sons' treachery, 'but I wasn't aware that they had the hearts of sheep.'

Carved on MacMurchey's tomb in Balnakeil Church are a skull and crossbones, and a man with a bow and arrow hunting a stag. The slab gives 1623 as the date of his death. The legend is that he paid £1,000 to be interred inside the church, because he was afraid that, if he was buried out in the graveyard, his grave would be desecrated by his enemies.

The church, at the very end of the road that leads west out of Durness, is a tranquil ruin now. Opposite, across a little burn, is the monumental Balnakeil House. The present building is Georgian, but an earlier dwelling was a haunt of the first Lord Reay, who came over from Tongue at certain times throughout the year to preside over criminal courts. The condemned were hanged nearby at Loch Croispol.

In 1991, in the dunes by Balnakeil beach, the bones were found of a Viking boy, twelve or thirteen years old. Along with his remains were grave goods, including a sword and a shield, amber and glass beads, gaming pieces, and a ring and comb made out of bone. Beyond the beach to the north is Faraid Head, where visitors come to watch nesting seabirds, thousands upon thousands of them, including guillemots, razorbills, fulmars and puffins.

Balnakeil beach is a beautiful stretch of sand, decorated with thin lines of tiny, pastel-coloured shells left behind by the retreating tide. Standing on the beach and looking west, you are facing Cape Wrath, the most north-westerly part of Britain. It's been called one of our last great wildernesses, and is also, paradoxically, a Ministry of Defence and NATO military training range.

'Wrath', pronounced with a short 'a', derives from the Old Norse *hvarf*, which means 'turning point': the place where Viking ships coming from Shetland and Orkney would turn south for the Western Isles, the Isle of Man, Dublin, and beyond. Before the Stevenson lighthouse was built in 1828, this was a hazardous place for mariners. It was off Cape Wrath that the smuggler Robert Honyman was drowned, together with his only son.

But that's another story, for another time…

# Afterword

The modern European fascination with folk tales and legends began in earnest with the publication, in Germany in 1812, of Jacob and Wilhelm Grimm's *Kinder- und Hausmärchen* (Nursery and Household Tales). Many of these fireside stories were very old, and capable of travelling across cultural and linguistic borders with ease. Though they were passed around primarily by being told aloud, they had also appeared in printed collections, for example in Charles Perrault's didactic *Mother Goose* stories of 1697, and in *The Arabian Nights' Entertainment* of 1706, and earlier they had been appropriated by, among others, Chaucer and Boccaccio. The work of the Grimm brothers was, at least, partly inspired by a burgeoning notion among intellectuals that the cultural bedrock of a nation's character could be found in the entertainments of its commonest people, the peasantry or 'folk', and it directly influenced collectors in other parts of Europe to go out and look for equivalent stories from their own countries.

In response to this enthusiasm, collections of traditional stories began to be published in Scotland. Particularly important, among many, are Robert Chambers' *Popular Rhymes of Scotland*, first published in 1826, which includes Scots versions of old 'wonder tales' of the kind favoured by the Grimms; and J.F. Campbell's Victorian collection *Popular Tales of the West Highlands*, which gathers together stories in Gaelic, mainly from Argyll and the Inner Hebrides. Recordings from the vast repertoire of Scottish traditional tales, in both Scots and Gaelic, were made by workers at the School of Scottish Studies, founded by Edinburgh University in 1951; transcriptions of many of the recordings appear in the magazine *Tocher*, and they can also be heard online on the Tobar an Dualchais website. Donald Smith's *Storytelling Scotland* gives a good overview of developments from early times up to the end of the twentieth century.

The opening of the Scottish Storytelling Centre in 1992 was a response to a growing interest in live storytelling. This book is a product of that same interest, coming out of my own experiences as a storyteller and as an organiser of storytelling events, and reflecting my enthusiasm for linking story to place. Nevertheless, it's important to repeat what I said earlier; that, although most of the stories in the collection have found homes in the places in which I've located them, versions may be found elsewhere, sometimes far afield. And it's important to emphasise that these are my own re-tellings. The notes that follow aren't intended to be comprehensive, but I hope they will be useful to the reader who is keen to find out more about the individual stories and to do some general reading. The order of paragraphs follows the sections of the book.

The story of The Flying Princess is found in many different versions across the Highlands; one says that she is buried in the graveyard at Kildonan on the Scoraig Peninsula. The tales of the Glenmore Giants come from Affleck Gray's *Legends of the Cairngorms*. I included Margaret and the Three Gifts here because it fits in so well, but the story is an enigma. Alec Williamson knows it, and I've heard a version told in Gaelic, but I'm convinced it's a literary creation which knowingly brings together different aspects of fairy belief. Whatever its origin, it's a great story to tell. Lizanne Henderson and Edward J. Cowan's *Scottish Fairy Belief: A History* is a comprehensive treatment of the theme. *The Gaelic Otherworld*, Ronald Black's edition of writings by John Gregorson Campbell, is a rich exploration of supernatural traditions in the Highlands and Islands in the latter half of the nineteenth century.

Elizabeth Sutherland's *Ravens and Black Rain* has information about the Brahan Seer, and about the second sight in general. The Golden Bowl was popular among storytellers some years ago. I don't know its origin, but I like to tell it about King Brude of the Picts. Columba's encounters with Brude and his priests, and with the Loch Ness monster, are recorded in Adomnan's *Life of St Columba*. The words of Hugh MacNally and Angus Grant can be heard in From Sea to Sea, a journey in sound along the Great Glen which Mairi MacArthur and I recorded and put together in 2001. Big Sandy of the Goblin is taken from Edward Ellice's *Place-Names of Glengarry and Glenquoich*, and The Blue-Eyed One is from a version in Mary MacKellar's 'Legends and Traditions of Lochaber' in the *Transactions of the Gaelic Society of Inverness*, vol. xvi.

It's interesting to compare this version of The Boy and the Blacksmith with an earlier one, recorded by Duncan Williamson in 1982, which appears in *A Thorn in the King's Foot*, a collection of Duncan's stories edited by Linda Williamson. The story of the origin of the Highland midgies is popular with Scottish storytellers. I've heard fine versions from Lawrence Tulloch of Shetland and Ross-shire's Janet MacInnes; I adapted it for Applecross. J.H. Dixon's *Gairloch*, which was first published in 1886, has the story of the Gille Dubh, as well as many other tales from Wester Ross. The Stalker, which is an old, international story, is adapted from a version in Campbell's *Popular Tales*. Big Hughie Kilpatrick also appears in Campbell, and a historical tradition has him as a survivor of the Battle of Flodden.

Alec Williamson's life is explored at length in Timothy Neat's two books *The Summer Walkers* and *When I was Young*. The story of The Lady of Ardvreck is taken from Hugh Miller's *Scenes and Legends of the North of Scotland*.

Alan Bruford and Donald A. MacDonald's *Scottish Traditional Tales*, an invaluable source of stories, has a Perthshire version of The Three Advices from Andrew Stewart, as well as a translation from the Gaelic telling of The Wren by Ailidh Dall. The Wee Boy and the Minister belongs to an old, international story type where the correct answering of riddles, or failure to do so, can sometimes save a life. Homer is said to have died of chagrin when he was unable to solve the riddle of the hunter.

Almost all of The King of the Cats is true. Finn MacCool – I've used the Anglicised spelling – is a famous Irish hero whose exploits have taken root in the Highlands and Islands.

In *Scenes and Legends*, Hugh Miller writes in a rich literary style which is wonderful to read aloud, but which also makes the stories quite long in print. I've tried here, with trepidation, to take them back to something like fireside versions.

The stories of Paul and Anthony, the first Desert Fathers, were originally told by their contemporaries, St Jerome and St Athanasius. In a number of the many stories of wind witches similar to that of Stine Bheag, the witch gives the sailors a thread which is knotted in three places, with the instruction not to untie the third knot until they arrive home. It's an old story. There is a version in Book X of Homer's *Odyssey*.

The Lady of Balconie is from Hugh Miller's *Scenes and Legends*. The curious tale of The Harbour Witch is taken from an article which appeared in the *Northern Times* on 8 April 1960.

The Seal Killer is one of my favourites. It appears in the splendid early collection, W. Grant Stewart's *The Popular Superstitions and Festive Amusements of the Highlanders of Scotland* of 1823.

There are many versions of How the Sea Became Salt. I've heard it from Tom Muir of Orkney and the Swedish story-teller Jerker Fahlström, among others. A vivid account of Essie Stewart's early life is given in *The Summer Walkers*. There's another Highland Traveller version of The Death of Ossian in Bruford and MacDonald's *Scottish Traditional Tales*. Donald Mackay appears in Revd George Sutherland's *Folklore Gleanings and Character Sketches* of 1937, as well as in the more recent *Tales of the North Coast* by Alan Temperley, which is a rich collection of stories from the far north. The story of the minister's heart and the Highwayman is given in Gunn and Mackay's *Sutherland and the Reay Country* of 1897.

Finally, may I recommend David Thomson's *The People of the Sea*, an account of his quest through Scotland, the Northern and Western Isles, and Ireland, searching for stories of selkies and other supernatural ocean dwellers; a magical bringing together of auto-biography, a sense of place, encounters with storytellers, and the stories themselves.

# GUIDE TO GAELIC PRONUNCIATION

The following is a simplified guide to the approximate pronunciations of some of the Gaelic names and words in the text, given in the order in which they occur. Note the 'ch' sounds as in the Scottish word 'loch'; and 'g' is hard, as in 'girl'. In the text, for most landscape features, apart from the instances below, I have used the spellings given on Ordnance Survey maps. I've also used the Anglicised versions of Fionn mac Cumhaill and Oisin – Finn MacCool and Ossian.

Ailidh Dall – _alee daal_
Dòmhnull Mòr – _donnal more_
Lochan Uaine – _loch-an oo-an-ya_
sgian dubh – _skee-an doo_
Bodach Làmh Dheirg – _bottach larve yerak_
Daoine Sìth – _doon-ya shee_
Sìthean – _shee-an_
Coinneach Odhar – _coin-yach oar_
each uisge – _ech oosh-ka_
Alasdair Mòr a'Bhòchdain – _alastair more a-voch-kan_
Caochan Glac a'Bhòchdain – _koochan glak a-voch-kan_
Gormshuil – _gorrum-hool_
Bealach – _bee-yaluch_

Sgùrr a'Chaorachain – _skoor a choor-uchan_
Bodach Stabhais – _bottach sta-veesh_
Gille Dubh – _gillie doo_
Uisdean Mòr Mac 'Ille Phàdruig – _oosh-jen more mac-illy fad-rik_
Fuath – _foo-a_
Rheguile – _ray-gool_
Glutan – _glutton_
Aonghas Donn – _innis down_
Stine Bheag – _steena vek_
Para Naomh-clèireach – _para nerv clairuch_
Biorach a'Bhuidheag – _beeruch a-vooyak_
Cailleach – _kye-yuch_